Alekhine's Anguish

ALEKHINE'S ANGUISH

A Novel of the Chess World

by

CHARLES D. YAFFE

McFarland & Company, Inc., Publishers
Jefferson, North Carolina, and London

Cover art by Stephen Shoemaker

Library of Congress Cataloguing-in-Publication Data

Yaffe, Charles D., 1910–
 Alekhine's anguish : a novel of the chess world / by Charles
D. Yaffe.
  p. cm.
  ISBN 0-7864-0695-X (softcover : 50# alkaline paper) ∞
  1. Alekhine, Alexander, 1892–1946—Fiction. I. Title.
PS3575.A28A79   1999
813'.54—dc21   99-31429
                                                                       CIP
British Library Cataloguing-in-Publication data are available

Manufactured in the United States of America

*McFarland & Company, Inc., Publishers
 Box 611, Jefferson, North Carolina 28640
  www.mcfarlandpub.com*

Author's Note

The real Alexander Alekhine had an eventful life. A number of situations which take place in this novel were suggested by actual occurrences. Many of the characters bear the names of individuals with whom he was involved. On the other hand, several characters with important roles in the plot, and the types of personalities portrayed for all concerned, including the protagonist, are purely imaginary. This a work of fiction.

Charles D. Yaffe
Summer 1999

Prologue

He looks up, expressionless. "Yes?"

"Tomorrow's scheduled executions."

Lenin puts down his pen and extends his hand for the dozen sheets.

The young aide stands there, wondering how a man twice his age can keep going hour after hour, day after day, week after week. Does he never rest?

Though it doesn't show, Lenin is tired. He feels the effects of another long and stressful day; a day like every other day for as long as he can recall. More than thirty of his forty-nine years spent in unending controversy, struggle, civil war; sometimes in Russia, sometimes in flight, sometimes in exile. No wonder his body is beginning to protest.

He scans the top sheet. Black marketing. Death by firing squad. He nods, signs his approval, hands it back, and looks at the next one. Asleep while on guard duty at an armory. Returning it with his signature, he picks up the following sheet. After a glance, his eyes narrow. He reads it carefully, pauses, sets it aside. When the remaining orders have been approved without questions, he returns to it and reads it again.

"Alekhine? Alexander Alekhine?" he asks, looking up.

"Yes?"

"What more do you know about the charges?"

"No more than what you see. Possession of a large stock of subversive materials."

Lenin lights a cigarette, inhales, strokes his beard with his right hand, while each finger of the other in turn is pressed against the desktop time and again. Smoke curls out of his nostrils. After a long moment,

1

he says, "We'll hold up action on this one. I want to look into it. Is there anything else urgent?"

"Nothing that can't wait until tomorrow."

"Good. You can leave now." And with a sudden smile, "Go find yourself some diversion for the evening."

Alone, still holding the execution order, he walks over to a window of the Kremlin and stares for a long time at the 1918 night sky over Moscow.

One

"I don't like the idea," his mother said.

"But why?" The anguish in his eyes distressed her.

His father set his brandy glass on the table beside his easy chair and raised his eyes from the letter he was examining. "Your mother is right. This is no time to go to Germany. The situation there is too muddled. We're watching it very closely."

"Are you saying there could be war?"

"That's not certain, but foreigners would be wise to stay away from there until we're sure Wilhelm comes to his senses."

He turned back to his mother. "But nothing could happen right away, could it? This is just for a couple of weeks. Please, this is my great chance to prove that I really belong at the top!"

"You've already proved it," his father said. "Even the tsar made that clear when he gave you the title of grandmaster."

Scornful, Alex whirled to face him. "Who gave him that authority? The tsar doesn't speak for the whole world. It takes more than one good performance to earn acceptance, and this is the perfect opportunity to show it wasn't an accident. If I don't show up, what I did here will be forgotten or considered a fluke. I may never get another chance as good as this!"

"There will be other invitations next year."

"Yes," the pitch of his voice rising almost to a screech as he glared at his father, "but maybe by then there really will be a war and, if not, I'll be stuck in law school, and won't have time to prepare or get away!"

Resigned to her usual role of peacemaker between them, his mother said, "And this will be finished before classes begin?"

"Yes. I'll get back with ten days to spare."

"Okay," she said, yielding with a sigh. "I suppose it will be all right. But if the news says war could begin, promise you'll leave and come home at once, even if the tournament isn't finished."

"Don't worry, I promise." Delighted, he threw his arms around his mother and squeezed her, kissing her ears, eyes and cheeks, and exclaiming, "Thank you, Mother, you're an angel!" Snatching the letter from his father's grasp, Alex dashed out of the room, collided with Zelda, the housekeeper, but grabbed her in time to keep them both from falling. Alex lifted Zelda up and whirled her around before setting her down, with a peck on the cheek, and rushing up the broad stairway to his room.

His father shook his head in disgust. "Sometimes I think he will never grow up. It's past time he should be preparing for life."

"He's smart, and he'll be successful at whatever he chooses to do. Meanwhile, let him enjoy himself a little."

Adding more brandy to his glass, his father muttered, "You've never denied him anything. This is another example. A foolish waste of money."

"Look who's talking," she replied, her tone etched with scorn, and snatched the decanter from him to pour her own generous refill.

The sparkle from the rays of the mid–July sun on the lake matched his spirits as he entered the impressive ballroom where the Nineteenth Congress of the Deutscher Schachbundes was being held to observe the 1914 fiftieth anniversary of the Mannheim chess club.

The tournament director, a bald, overweight, middle-aged man named Gustav Hoffmann, interrupted his conversation with someone when he saw Alex approach the registration table. "Alekhine! I'm so happy that you have come."

"Thanks, I'm glad to be here, and can't wait to play you again."

"No chance of that. Once was enough. I'm quite satisfied to just be running the show. By the way, do you know Antonio Lupi, the new champion of Portugal?"

Before Alex could reply, Lupi, a slender, bright-eyed man, with thick, curly, black hair, thrust out his hand and, continuing in the German he had been using with Hoffmann, said, "Alekhine? It's a pleasure to meet you. I've been reading about your exceptional exploits."

The physical contrast between Alex and the others was marked. Blond, his hair growing in a sharp widow's peak, at six foot three Alex towered a half-foot above them. Replying in careful but correctly pronounced Portuguese, he said, "The pleasure is mine. It's a privilege to meet any nation's champion."

"Someone who speaks my language! How wonderful! From now on, you have only to ask and it shall be yours!" he exclaimed with delight as he gave Alex's hand an enthusiastic shake. Turning to Hoffmann, and in German, he said, "His accomplishments extend to languages, as well as chess. Outside my country it is rarely that I meet someone who speaks Portuguese. I shall not let this young man out of my sight. I am his friend for life!"

Hoffmann was called to the telephone before he could respond. As Lupi turned back to Alex, a malodorous cloud shot between them, and they each felt a strong blow on their backs as a voice bellowed, "Welcome, fellow woodpushers!"

"I'd know that stinking cigar anywhere. How are you, Frank?" Alex said in English, grinning, as he turned to shake hands with a tall, brown-haired man in his mid-thirties.

"Here I be to get my revenge!" After squeezing Alex's hand, he turned to Lupi. "How's the pride of Lisbon?"

"Intimidated to be in such distinguished company as two 'grandmasters' at once. It's a privilege to see you again, Mr. Marshall."

"Golly, I didn't know that word of our exalted status had spread so far. Did you hire a publicity agent to spread the word, Alex?"

"No. Now we have the job of proving we deserve it. What happens when some 'patzer' beats us?"

"Then, I guess, we earn the new title of 'patsy'," said Marshall, coughing violently, as his laugh and cigar smoke collided in this throat.

Alex pounded him on the back and, when the coughing had stopped, said, "Let's go outside and enjoy the view. A little fresh air will do us all good, too."

As they stood at the lake's edge, he said, "How about the rest of our illustrious group? Will they be here?"

"Only Tarrasch. Lasker and Capa are afraid to face me again."

Alex chuckled. "It isn't you they are afraid of, it's your cigars."

"Well, all's fair in love and chess. Don't you agree, Lupi?"

5

"Yes, unfortunately, but I'm thinking of starting a movement to change the rules, so that a player must give up a piece every time he lights a cigar."

"Count me in," said Alex.

"Okay, okay, let's change the subject. Tell me, how did you fellows learn to speak such good English? Lupi?"

"Blame it on three years at the London School of Economics."

"Really? I'm impressed. Now about your German and English, Alex? You sound as much like a native here as Herr Hoffmann, and your English is just as good, though you do sound more like a bloody English lord than an American businessman."

"Oh, that was my mother's doing. She had me tutored in German, French and English, starting when I was only seven or eight. Then I majored in language studies in college."

"His Portuguese is excellent, too," said Lupi.

"It needs more practice. I'll have to spend some time in your country."

"That would be great. Just let me know when you want to come."

"Thanks, I shall."

"Was there a special reason why the 'grandmaster' title was awarded at the Moscow tourney?" Lupi asked.

"It was a surprise to me," said Marshall. "Maybe Alex knows why."

"No, it was a surprise to me, too. Maybe since the tsar put up the prize money, he thought the publicity of adding those new titles would attract more attention to his generosity. He likes favorable publicity."

"So do I," Marshall commented. "But I wouldn't think he needed it."

"Well, it's just a theory of mine. I don't happen to share my parents' enthusiasm for him, so maybe I'm prejudiced."

"Imagine my surprise," the American told Lupi, "to learn that the couple with the tsar at our closing banquet were his parents. Your folks travel in upper circles, don't they, Alex?"

"Well, my father happens to hold an influential position in the government."

"Don't knock it, boy, some day it could come in handy."

Sensing that Alex seemed uncomfortable with the topic, Lupi said, "Let's see, Lasker and Capablanca finished first and second, didn't they? You two were next, weren't you?"

"Alex was next, but Tarrasch beat me out for fourth prize by a half-point. Fortunately, the tsar included me in his anointment of the chess hierarchy."

"I was surprised to read that Capablanca lost to Lasker in the final round. The way he's been playing, I didn't think that would happen."

Marshall gave a short laugh. "Well, I can tell you what they say happened. Up until ten minutes before the game started, Capa is said to have been playing in bed with some Russian beauty, and didn't have his mind on chess when he got there. Isn't that right, Alex?"

"That's the story going around. I might add that I overheard my parents whispering that the beauty involved was probably the special lady friend of the grand duke. Russians love to gossip about scandals, particularly those concerning the nobility."

"Shucks, we don't have nobility in the U.S., but people get similar kicks from scandals involving our rich and famous. It's the same everywhere, isn't it, Lupi?"

"Of course, it happens in my country all the time."

"Nice job, Alex! You've got first prize just about locked up, after beating Tarrasch like that. With a two-point lead I don't think anyone will catch you."

"Thanks Frank. Maybe not, as long as I don't get over-confident."

"You won't. You're smart enough." Marshall looked around to see what games were still in progress. "I wonder how our Portuguese friend is doing against Bogul. Let's take a look."

They walked over to a game still going on. Lupi was playing Ewfim Boguljubov, another strong master from Russia. It was the first day of August, and the last games of the eleventh round were nearing completion.

The cocoon of quiet enveloping the contests still in progress suddenly vaporized as the front doors burst open, boots thudded, a shouted "Achtung!" thundered from wall to wall, and the startled occupants of the hall stared at the young German officer who strode in, followed by a squad of rifle-bearing soldiers.

"What is the meaning of this?" the outraged Hoffmann demanded, bustling up to the officer. "You are disturbing an important international competition!"

"The meaning is simple. This affair is finished. Germany is now at war with her enemies—a much more important international competition. No one is to leave here until we have established their identities. Citizens of enemy states will be detained. Any Germans here who are in the armed forces or reserves will report at once to their units for duty. All other German nationals will return to their homes without delay. Nationals of other countries will arrange to leave Germany within twenty-four hours. Is that clear?" Before anyone could speak, he added, "Who is in charge here?"

"I am," said Hoffmann.

"Very well. I shall want an office where we can interview everyone present."

Hoffmann thought a moment, then pointed, "Over there is one which may be suitable. It has a desk, a table and chairs. There is also a telephone in the room."

The lieutenant followed him to the indicated room, looked around, and said it would do.

"How many people are here?"

"There are seventy-three players, eighteen in the master group, and fifty-five in the lower-rated contests."

"Is there an audience?"

"Yes, I would estimate that there are between sixty and seventy paid attendees at the moment."

"Hmm. That means about one hundred and fifty to check. It will take awhile, I'd guess at least five or six hours. Are all the attendees local people?"

"I think so. There could be a few from out of town, but I believe they are all Germans."

"Okay, we'll get them out of here first. It will be a few minutes before we are ready to see any of them. Corporal," he ordered, calling to the uniformed man posted at the door, "go with Herr Hoffmann and assemble all of the people who were just spectators. Have them form a line starting near the entrance to this room."

The instant the officer had disappeared with Hoffmann, the trickle of words began, swelling into a torrential cascade of competing sounds— shouts, groans, whispers, laughter—reaching a crescendo when a group

8

near a wall burst into "Deutschland über Alles" rendered with more enthusiasm than harmony. Most of those contestants who had still been playing stopped—some sat in stunned silence, others joined audience members who were milling around, searching for acquaintances or probable allies with whom to exchange opinions—but, oblivious of the situation, the players at two of the boards calmly went on with their games. The non–Germans in the hall—possibly twenty-five in number—were silent, or conversed in quiet tones only with fellow-countrymen, anger, anxiety, and apprehension apparent in their faces. In contrast were the excited exchanges between many of the Germans, though those facing the prospect of active military duty, or fathers of sons with similar situations, generally displayed less enthusiasm.

The cacophonous racket subsided when the corporal bellowed, "Achtung! Quiet, everyone! There is to be no more unnecessary noise. Now, pay attention! All of you who were just paid members of the audience will form a line along the walls, starting here where I am standing. The rest of you will restrain yourselves and wait further orders."

Hoffmann asked the corporal a question, then turned to the assemblage and announced, "You might as well sit down, gentlemen, this is going to take several hours."

Instead, a number of the contestants rushed up to him, all talking at once. "Which countries are at war?"

"How are we supposed to get home?"

"Can we finish the tournament somewhere else?"

"Can I notify my wife?"

"What about the prizes?"

"Will our return tickets be honored for earlier departure?"

Hoffmann held up both hands. "Gentlemen, gentlemen, please, you know as much as I do. I suppose the lieutenant is acting under orders, and that means the tournament will not be allowed to continue. As for your questions, they plan to interview each of you, and I imagine they will give you the answers then. Meanwhile, we can only be patient."

"If the tourney is over, you ought to award prizes based on the present standings," said Marshall, one of the group clustered around the besieged director. "We've done our part and should be paid accordingly."

"Yes," one of the others chimed in. "You're honor bound to pay us what we've earned."

Hoffmann cleared his throat. "Under the circumstances, I shall have to find out whether I am permitted to give money to any of you, particularly to those of you from other countries. If he will spare me the time, I'll go and see whether the lieutenant can authorize such awards. I must tell you, though, that the prizes will have to be smaller than those announced, as we will not have the revenue expected from admission to the six cancelled rounds. There just isn't enough in the till to pay in full."

In response to sounds of protest, he added, "Gentlemen, you must accept that contractual arrangements are bound to be affected by acts of war. However, I am a man of honor, and will do my best. Now, with your permission, I'll see what the authorities have to say."

Alex sat alone, submerged in gloom and guilt. He could visualize the scene at home—his mother worried, her frame of mind not helped by his father's ranting at her for agreeing to his trip to Mannheim. There was no telling how long or where these arrogant Germans would hold him, or what problems there would be in getting home after his release. Most of all, his depressed mood came because the recognition of his outstanding performance here would be buried by the avalanche of war news. It had all been for nothing.

These thoughts were interrupted when Marshall joined him at the table and reported," Hoffmann is trying to find out whether prizes can be awarded. If so, you could pick up a nice piece of change."

Alex shrugged. "How long do you think this war will last?"

"Hard to tell. It could drag on for several months. On the other hand, it may be over in less than a week."

"Will you go right back to New York?"

"As fast as I can get there. I want to get as far from Europe as possible, as soon as possible. I just hope ship schedules won't be disrupted."

"Will you do me a favor?" Alex asked, as he began writing on a scrap of paper torn from a pocket notebook. "As soon as you get home, if the war is still going on, will you send a message the quickest way possible to my mother at this address? Tell her that I'm okay, but that they are detaining me, and I would welcome anything she could do to get me released."

"Do you think your father could manage that?"

"Not him, but if anyone can, she will." He handed his friend a hundred marks. "There may be some expense getting word to her. If there's any left you can give it to me the next time we see each other."

"Shucks, Alex, I'll be glad to do it, but you don't need to lend me money."

"Take it. I have plenty."

"Okay, and it's the first thing I'll do when I hit New York."

They watched, as the first man lined up against the wall entered the lieutenant's office. It was almost five minutes before he emerged and was allowed to leave the building. It was the same for the next man.

"This is going to take forever," Marshall muttered. "We might as well play some chess."

Alex agreed. There was nothing better to do.

An hour later, Hoffmann interrupted their game. "Gentlemen, I have been allowed to award prizes. I'm sorry they are not as much as planned. All have been reduced proportionately. Herr Alekhine, your prize for being in first place is seven hundred marks. Herr Marshall, your reward for being in a triple tie for fourth place is eighty-seven marks." Handing them the cash, he added, "I have been assured that this money will not be taken away from you."

"I guess we have to be thankful for small favors," grumbled Marshall, watching Hoffmann as he paid some of the others.

Alex stuffed the money in his wallet. Maybe it could help him get out of Germany.

The night dragged on. It was past midnight when nationals from the non-belligerent nations were lined up along the wall to await their interrogations. An hour later Marshall emerged from his interview and, under escort by a soldier, was only able to give Alex a small wave as he went by.

At three o'clock, the lieutenant came out of his office and spoke to the weary group remaining, "Is there anyone here who is not from England, France or Russia?"

No one responded.

"In that case, we shall continue later. Meanwhile, make yourselves comfortable if you can. You will stay here for the rest of the night." He then marched out, but the armed guards at the doors remained.

Two

They are eight: five Russians, two French citizens, and a lone Englishman. The black bread, cheese, and potato soup they are devouring at eleven in the morning is their first nourishment in almost twenty-four hours. Several hours earlier, electric power to the building has been cut off. The rain beating against the windows reduces the scant daylight, transforming the vast hall into a cavern as dim as their spirits. Conversation among them has long since stopped. The guards are unresponsive to their questions, and the lieutenant, when he finally interviews each of them, volunteers no information, and leaves the building again. They can only pace the floor or sit and ponder on what to expect.

Their wait ends in mid-afternoon. They are loaded into a canvas-covered truck, equipped with a bench on each side. After a long, slow, bumpy ride, soldiers escort them into a large, brick house which stands in the center of grounds spacious enough to isolate it from its neighbors. The dusty, unfurnished interior, grimy windows, and peeling wallpaper attest that no one has occupied it for some time.

Another truck follows them. From it come straight chairs and plain tables which the soldiers leave in the middle of the parlor. Next, they bring in folding, canvas cots which are stacked in the upstairs hall leading to several bedrooms. Eight lightweight blankets are dumped beside the cots.

A guard checks to verify that water—a slow, rusty trickle—will emerge from faucets in the kitchen and upstairs bathroom, and that the one toilet flushes. There being no heat, it is immaterial that there are no handles on the hot water faucets.

The kitchen is unequipped except for a wood-burning cookstove and a supply of its fuel, but the soldiers add a mop, broom, bucket, two oil lanterns, and boxes containing plates, cups and eating utensils, as well as pots, pans, and some kitchen knives and spoons. Another box holds towels, toothbrushes and soap.

Finally, they bring in some loaves of bread, a sack of potatoes, some onions and turnips, a bucket of lard, two large sausages, a bag of coffee, another of sugar, and some salt and pepper.

Their task completed, the sergeant in charge of the detachment places a couple of packs of cigarettes, a can of tobacco and two decks of cards on a table, smiles, and says, "Make yourselves at home, men. We'll be in touch." He orders his men out, locks the door from the outside, and posts guards at the front and rear entrances.

The eyes of the eight men followed the sergeant as he left, and remained on the door until they heard the key turn in the lock. Then, as if by signal, they looked at each other, as though for the first time. Except for chess they had little in common. They ranged in age up to sixty-six, with Alex, at twenty-one, the youngest. In general, their economic, social and educational backgrounds were similar in few instances. Alex was the only one in the group able to speak the languages of all three countries they represented.

When, after a pause, Boguljubov broke the silence, saying, "Suppose we look the place over, then we'd better sit down and get organized," the men from England and France wore blank expressions until Alex translated for them.

They climbed the stairs and found that the upper floor contained four bedrooms and the bathroom. While they were up there, they quickly agreed that the other Russians would use two of the bedrooms, the Frenchmen would share a third one, and Alex would room with the Englishman, who spoke neither French nor Russian.

Back downstairs, around a table, they selected Andreyov Vukov, the oldest of the group, a school teacher from Leningrad, to act as chairman for their meeting, with Alex given the job of interpreter.

The supplies left by their captors gave no clue as to when they might be released, but it was clear that preparation of meals and housekeeping would depend on their own efforts. Two of the group volunteered to prepare that evening's meal. To get it done before dark, they began work at once. Outside of getting the table set, and placing two cots and blankets in each bedroom, little more was attempted. The stew produced by the volunteers was eaten by lantern light without complaining. The preceding night having been largely a sleepless one, after each had rinsed his own dishes, they were all ready to turn in.

Following a breakfast of bread, sausage and coffee the next morning, the men reached decisions on the division of certain tasks, and started a list of items to be requested from their guardians.

There was a brief break in the monotony the second day after their arrival. A supply truck appeared bringing additional supplies of the same foods they had received before, but nothing else. The sergeant in charge of the delivery selected three of the internees to carry them into the house under guard.

"Could we have some other items the next time you come?" Alex asked the sergeant, at Vukov's request.

"It depends on what you want," was the answer. "Have a written list ready."

"We have one. Here it is. If we are to be kept here, we would particularly appreciate it if you could bring some chess sets the next time you come."

"I'll see what the captain has to say."

"I don't suppose you know how long we'll be held?"

The sergeant grinned. "No, but it may not be long. Our forces aren't meeting much opposition."

More food arrived forty-eight hours later, but without the chess sets. This time, the sergeant answered no questions on the progress of the war, leaving the group frustrated. Worse than the tedium was ignorance of what was happening. The only fragments of information they could glean came from examination of old newspapers used to wrap some of the supplies.

Two of the Russians drew lines on a table to form a chessboard, and wrote identifying letters on scraps of paper to serve as pieces.

Watching the first game played with this makeshift set, Alex commented, "I'd rather try playing blindfold."

"Can you play blindfold?" asked Boguljubov.

"I think so. Can you?"

"I've done it a few times."

"Let's try it!" said Alex, with the first enthusiasm he'd felt in days.

Their experiment was successful and, from then on, the two spent hours every day in a room by themselves engaged in satisfying battles. Within a short time, they both developed the ability to play almost as easily and quickly as when they had the customary equipment in front of them. A few of the others tried to play *sans voir* but soon gave up.

Though from different backgrounds—Boguljubov, round-faced and overweight, from peasant stock, had studied to become a priest, but gave it up to pursue an insecure professional career in chess—the two were drawn together by their passion for the game, as well as because they were the youngest in the group, with only three years difference in their ages.

On the ninth day two trucks appeared. This time, under supervision, the eight men loaded their furnishings into one truck, then boarded the other. From the position of the sun they could tell that they were headed south. Traffic on the narrow road was congested and slow. Much of it consisted of wagons pulled by farm animals. There were frequent stops to let military convoys pass. Choking dust and rural smells enveloped them for the first few hours, as they jounced along the rutted road. The dust subsided as it began to rain lightly, then with increasing intensity. The trucks began to slide and jog as the road turned into a sea of slop. On several occasions one or the other of the trucks became mired in the mud, and the passengers were unloaded to help get them moving again.

It was dusk when they reached a large farmhouse into which they carried their cots, blankets and towels. The group was set up in two adjoining rooms. One room was large enough to accommodate five of the men, with the other having just enough space for the remaining three. Each room had a small table on which there was a pitcher and wash basin. There was no running water in the house. Their trips to the outdoor privy were made under armed escort.

Three women and two men, a sullen couple with their son and daughters, lived there.

In two shifts, the internees were brought to the kitchen and served meals, not fancy, but welcome improvements over what had been sustaining them.

Their journey southward was resumed after two days. It ended, at last, on the outskirts of the city of Rastatt, east of the French border. Here they were installed much more comfortably in a small inn appropriated by the authorities. The beds in the already furnished rooms were far more satisfactory than the cots they had been using, and there were two bathrooms in which water flowed at a reasonable rate. There was even hot water a few hours each day.

They had use of a parlor containing a few old books and magazines, and a dining room where they were served reasonable food. They had access to all of the building, though their presence in the kitchen was not encouraged by the staff. Under supervision they were also allowed out into a walled court for an hour of exercise each day. In addition to the inn staff they found six other internees already in residence.

Three

Hearing the front door close, she jumped from her chair so quickly that some of the brandy splashed on her silk dress. "Any news?"

Grumpily, Victor Alekhine shook his head, poured from the decanter and drank, as he slumped into his chair. "Nothing."

"But, surely…"

"There's nothing that can be done about it now," he interrupted. "If you'd listened to me we wouldn't be worrying, because Alex wouldn't be in Germany!"

Angered, she snapped, "Not even as cannon fodder?"

He tossed off the remainder of his drink and said, "If so, it would at least be for an honorable reason."

"Honor be damned! I want my son back, and you babble about honor," she said, with a sob. "Is there no other way to find out where he is?"

"Can't you get it through that head of yours? All communications are tied up. My God! Our army is about to march on Prussia. Believe it or not, I have other responsibilities in the duma which are more important than a misplaced chess player, even one who happens to be my son. Whatever you think about honor, he should have been here to meet his responsibilities as a lieutenant in the reserves." He stood up, grabbed his hat, and left again for the legislative chamber where he was spending virtually all his waking hours.

As for his wife, though she devoted many hours in volunteer work for the Red Cross, her mind was only on Alex.

Weeks later, when the message from Frank Marshall finally arrived, she didn't bother to notify her husband. Instead, Alex's mother immediately had herself driven to her father's office, a place she had not visited since she was a little girl.

Dmitri Prokhoreff, her father, was an industrialist of considerable wealth. Some of this came from mines in Siberia yielding minerals essential for his production of an alloy of exceptional hardness. His principal customer for this alloy the past three years was the German navy. Only with this was it possible for them to produce submarines capable of extended service in the western Atlantic. Business was business, war or no war, and Prokhoreff was continuing shipments, though via a more circuitous route.

"Agnes?" he said, astonished, "what brings you here?"

"Papa, I just received this."

He read Marshall's message, scowled, then said, "Leave it to me."

From his neck—the circumference of which exceeded that of his head—a red flush rose and engulfed the face of the admiral in charge of naval procurement. He glared in disbelief at this visitor, the officer responsible for submarine production. "You mean to stand there and tell me that the work is stopping just because our goddamned army is holding a fucking chess player?"

"In a nutshell, that's the situation."

"Well, we will see about that!" he growled, erupting from his chair and heading for the door.

Alex was just finishing his breakfast, about six weeks after the forlorn chess group had been settled in Rastatt, when he was summoned to the parlor. A German army captain awaited him.

"Alekhine? You are Alexander Alekhine?" asked the officer, looking at him with undisguised interest.

"Yes, I am Alekhine."

"Do you have any other clothes or possessions?"

Alex shook his head.

"Come with me," he was ordered.

"Get in," his escort directed, when they reached a car where a soldier opened the door to the back seat. The captain spoke to the driver, then sat next to Alex.

As the car moved toward the city, a perplexed ghost of a smile on his face, he said, "I don't know who the hell you are, but somebody must love you, because I'm ordered to get you out of Germany as soon as possible."

Alex's hopes of release had faded early, and for weeks his mind had been filled with fanciful dreams of daring escapes. Realization of what the captain had just said set off such a furious pounding of his heart that he did not trust himself to speak.

Curious about this young man, the captain said, "May I ask what you were doing in Germany?"

"Playing chess," Alex replied, when he managed to regain his voice.

"Chess!"

"Yes, when the fighting started I was at an international tournament in Mannheim."

What a way to run a war, the captain reflected, shaking his head. "Where is your home?"

"Moscow."

"So, what will you do when you are released?"

"Report to my reserve unit, I suppose. I don't imagine I'll have any option."

"Would you rather not?"

"Of course. I think the whole business is stupid. What's all the killing going to accomplish?"

"If you feel that way, why did you join the reserves?"

"It was the only thing to do, according to my father."

"What would you like to do?"

"I'm going to be chess champion of the world."

Disconcerted by this bizarre response, the German decided to ask no more questions.

When they reached the railroad station the captain went in to arrange for transportation. There were no empty seats in the crowded waiting room, so they waited in the car for an hour until they were able to board the first train to Switzerland.

They left the train at Basel. The captain directed their taxi driver to take them to the Swiss United Bank, where he asked to see the managing director.

After a short wait, a portly, white-haired man appeared. "I am Henry Erdmann, the managing director. You wished to see me?"

The captain introduced himself and handed the banker some papers. Erdmann scanned these, then said, "Wait here a moment, please, Captain."

Taking Alex into his office, he said, "You are Alexander Alekhine?"

Alex nodded.

"Who is Dmitri Prokhoreff?"

"He is my grandfather, my mother's father."

A broad smile lit up Erdmann's face. He held out his hand. "We've been expecting you. Welcome to Switzerland! We are happy to see you. Please sit down. I'll be back as soon as I sign off with the captain."

Although several hours had gone by since he was told he was to be released, it was only now that he relaxed and felt he could really accept the fact. He was free. Life could begin again.

"Well," said Erdmann, when he rejoined Alex, "that must have been quite an experience. I understand you were held ever since the war began?"

"That's right."

"How did they treat you?"

"I suppose it could have been worse. We weren't beaten, or anything like that, but it wasn't something I would wish on anyone. Freedom is a wonderful experience."

"I can imagine. It's something most of us just take for granted."

"It's one thing I'll cherish from now on."

"I'm sure you will. Now, what can we do for you? I assume you would like to get home as soon as you can, but your grandfather recommends a roundabout way which he considers safest, even though it will be time-consuming. I've known him a long time, and respect his judgment. When he called me to expect you, he advised that you take a ship from Genoa to Lisbon, then use another from Lisbon to Norway, preferably Bergen. From there you can go by rail to Stockholm, then on to Tallin by water. You'd be in neutral vessels all the way, and only the last leg should have any possible risk. So far, the Germans haven't been bothering shipping in that vicinity. What do you think?"

"I'm glad to rely on what he suggests. We were kept in complete ignorance about what's going on. From what you say, I gather that the war is still in progress, but that's all I know."

"Well, we'll bring you up to date on that, and I'd like to hear about your experiences, but I'm sure you'd like to get settled first. I can recommend a hotel, and then we should consider doing something about your wardrobe. I don't suppose you have any money?"

"Yes, I do have about eight hundred German marks. They allowed me to keep the prize money I won in Mannheim."

"I'm surprised you've been able to hang on to it. I'll make inquiries about schedules and costs. If necessary, we can advance whatever additional funds you'll need. Meanwhile, I believe a few days here getting yourself back in the real world should be good for you."

"I can't tell you how much I appreciate what you are doing for me."

"I'm glad to do whatever I can. Your grandfather and I have been friends for many years. I'll get word to him right away that you are here safe and sound."

"Thank you. I know how relieved my mother will be when he gives her the news."

Placing a call to Hotel Fairview, Erdmann identified himself and asked that they provide Alex with their best room, and that he would be arriving in a few minutes.

"After you are settled in the room," he told Alex, "there is a men's clothier, Strauss's, in the same block, where you can get everything you will need. Have them place the charges on my personal account. I will notify them to do so."

"But I have money," Alex protested.

"Hold on to it. You will need it later."

Because of the banker's call, the receptionist at the small hotel ignored Alex's scruffy appearance, welcomed him warmly, and personally escorted him to his large, comfortably furnished room.

As it was getting late in the afternoon, Alex only took time to scrub his hands and face, and to shave with a razor the receptionist had lent him before going on to the clothier. There he acquired a suitable new wardrobe, which they promised to deliver to him before evening. He then searched out a store where he was able to buy a pocket-size chess set suitable for travel.

Back in his room he pegged some of the pieces into the appropriate squares, and spent an hour examining various options in a tricky endgame situation while luxuriating in a hot bath, his first in many weeks.

Clothed in new suit, shirt, tie and shoes, he entered the restaurant adjoining the hotel. The first tastes of dinner and the wine he ordered were pure ecstasy, but while finishing everything as though famished, interest in the meal faded as the position on his pocket-size board reclaimed Alex's total attention.

"That's an interesting position," his waiter commented, when he brought the tab for the meal.

Alex looked up. "You play?"

"Some."

"Is there a chess club here?"

"Yes, two blocks down, across the street, above the tailor shop."

It was a dingy room. Games were in progress at two of the six boards set up on tables consisting of doors resting on sawhorses. There were eleven straight chairs in the room, no three alike. Aside from a bulletin board supported by a tripod, there were no other furnishings. Light on the table was concentrated by green, circular, metal reflectors above each of the four electric lightbulbs suspended by cords emerging from the ceiling. Even during the day, little light would penetrate the two small windows, which gave no evidence of ever having been washed.

A glance at the disposition of the pieces in one of the games told Alex that the players—both appeared in their late teens—understood little about the basic principles of sound chess play.

The men involved in the other game were in their forties or fifties, as were most of their audience of five, two of which were seated next to the players, while the others stood grouped behind one of the contestants. One of them nodded to acknowledge Alex's presence when he posted himself behind the other player. Almost everyone at the table was puffing either a cigar or pipe.

The man seated in front of Alex carried on a running monologue when it was his move, explaining to himself what terrible fate would befall him if he used a certain tactic. His opponent was silent, spending the time lighting one wood match after another, vainly attempting to revive the ashes in his pipe, while several of the kibitzers offered facetious advice to the player across the table. Alex noted that, after all the discussion, the man usually made good moves. Eventually, with a sound of disgust, the opponent knocked his king down and began scraping the unresponsive ashes from his pipe.

22

The man who had nodded to Alex said, "You are a visitor?"

"Yes, just looking around."

"Care to play a game?"

Alex hesitated, then said, "All right."

Once they were seated the man picked up pawns of opposite colors, put his hands briefly under the table, then presented his closed fists. When Alex pointed to the left one both were opened to show he had chosen the black pieces.

Before making the first move his opponent put out his hand, saying, "My name is Franz Regner."

"Alekhine, Alexander Alekhine," he responded, shaking hands.

"Alekhine?" asked one of the seated men. "From Russia?"

"Yes."

"I thought I read that the Germans were holding you."

"They were, but I managed to get away."

As the others looked at him with curiosity, his questioner said, "Men, I think we have one of the world's strongest players in our midst. Am I right?"

Alex smiled slightly.

"Didn't you finish third, just behind Lasker and Capablanca in that big tournament a few months ago?"

The smile widened as he dipped his head.

"My God! And I offer to take you on?" Regner said, with a moan.

"I'll be glad to play you. Go ahead and move."

Everyone in the room watched as he disposed of Regner in little more than a dozen moves. After some admiring comments, someone asked, "How did you get away from the Germans?"

Alex hesitated, then said, "I think it is best that I not go into details. Let's just say that there are sometimes ways to influence events."

"Such as money?"

Alex grinned. "As I said, it is probably not advisable to say any more at the present time."

"How long will you be here?" asked Regner.

"I'm not certain. Possibly about a week."

"Would you be willing to give a simultaneous exhibition?"

Alex thought about it for a moment. He had never done one.

"We would pay you, of course."

"How many boards do you have in mind?"

Regner huddled with the others, then said, "We have about forty members. If it were held this Friday evening we think at least a dozen probably would be willing to pay two francs for the opportunity to play you, and the same number would pay one franc just to watch. We'd be willing to guarantee you a minimum of thirty-five francs."

Alex drew a breath, as he calculated. "Okay, as long as there are no more than twenty boards. What time would we start?"

After another conference, Regner suggested seven o'clock, which Alex said was satisfactory.

❖ ❖ ❖

Word of the exhibition spread rapidly and most of the club members plus several others of the chessplaying community were there when Alex arrived Friday evening. Additional tables had been set up and were connected to form a horseshoe shape. A number of additional chairs had also been brought in. There was also a card table on which were a pitcher of water and a carafe of coffee for Alex's use. Eighteen individuals were seated around the outer rim of the tables, with chess pieces in place on their boards.

After a brief discussion with Alex, the club president spoke. "Friends, I am glad to see so many of you here tonight, especially those of you who have not yet joined our club. I hope this get-together will inspire you to become members. We are privileged to have one of the finest chess players in the world here this evening, a young man who has just escaped from a dangerous and exhausting experience, having been captured when the war began, just as he was winning an important tournament in Mannheim. In spite of the months of stress and strain he went through until just this week, he has graciously agreed to demonstrate his abilities here. Because this exhibition will require a number of hours, he has asked me to be brief and just explain the rules. Mr. Alekhine will play White and Black on alternate boards, beginning with White on the first board. He will make just one move at a time at each board, and you will be expected to make your responding move as soon as he reaches you again. Are there any questions.?"

There being none, Alex stepped to the first board, shook hands with his opponent, asked his name, made his first move, and proceeded to the next board where, after a similar greeting, he made his answering move immediately after his opponent started the contest. His first circuit, even with the time for handshakes, was completed in just a minute. Alex kept up this pace for the first few times around the tables, scarcely hesitating before moving his piece. Most of the players were recording the moves and would soon find themselves pressed for time to write these and plan their next ones.

Once past the openings he occasionally began to pause for a few seconds before making a decision. During his eleventh circuit, one of his opponents, expression rueful, turned down his king. Alex smiled, shook his hand, lit a cigarette, and moved on. Fifteen minutes had elapsed since the exhibition started.

At the end of the first hour, by which time he was finishing his fourth cigarette, thirteen opponents still faced him. His speed of play slowed during the second hour, in which five more resigned or were checkmated.

Up to this point, he had only stopped a few times for a little water. Now, he poured himself a cup of coffee, which he carried in his left hand, sipping it when he stopped to ponder a move. At such times, unaware of the mannerism, the middle finger of his right hand would invariably press against the point of his widow's peak, as if to serve as a channel for the instructions his hand was to carry out.

Around nine-thirty, one of his competitors offered him a draw. Alex scrutinized the position, agreed and congratulated him, producing a buzz of excitement among the onlookers. The man at the next board hesitantly also offered a draw. Alex smiled, but shook his head. Watchers in that vicinity laughed, two rounds later, when Alex said, "Mate in one," as the man clapped his hand to his head in dismay.

The twelfth stroke of the clock in a nearby tower echoed through the room just before the last game ended, when the club champion decided to resign after sixty-four moves. Smiling, as he accepted the applause of the remaining twenty-odd spectators, Alex said, "Thank you, gentlemen. If there is some place nearby where we can still get something to eat, and possibly some wine, and there are any of you not yet ready for bed, I shall be glad to have you join me."

It was two-thirty before a small group, including the club champion, broke up after hearing Alex analyze several of the games, all of which he remembered completely, replaying each from the start, move by move. On returning to his room, Alex found sleep was slow coming after the stress of the evening. Until it arrived, he was content to lie there, reviewing his performance, in which he had not lost a game, with only three draws as minor blemishes.

Erdmann completed arrangements for Alex to sail the following week from Genoa to Lisbon. "Circumstances could change, so you'll have to do your own scheduling from there on. When you get to Lisbon, you should go to the Russian Embassy. They will be able to give advice about the situation, and can also help you arrange the rest of your trip. I have also established credit at a Lisbon bank, should you need additional funds."

"I don't know how I could have managed without all your help. I have no idea how long it would have taken me to get back and join my reserve unit, which I am sure has already been called into active duty. I know my parents appreciate what you have done as much as I do."

"What kind of reserve unit are you in?"

"I'm a lieutenant in an artillery battery."

"Are you anxious to see action?"

Alex grinned. "You bet. It should be exciting, and after my recent experiences I have some scores to settle."

Four

Alex had three days in Genoa before sailing. After a half-day sight-seeing, he happened upon a chess club, where he could be found during almost all of his waking hours until his ship was ready to leave.

The vessel was a freighter, but was equipped to carry a dozen passengers. Several of those on board lived in Lisbon. During meals, Alex pumped them for various kinds of information about the city. At other times, however, he kept largely to himself. When not in his bunk studying his pocket chess set he was pacing the deck or leaning against the rail, wondering about his future and how he might control it.

From what Alex had learned, he knew the general area where he wanted to find temporary lodging. He took care of this immediately after they docked in Lisbon, getting a room in a small, inexpensive hotel. As soon as he was settled he made his way on foot to the Russian Embassy and identified himself. Word of his presence spread rapidly. Within a few minutes he found his hand being shaken by Ambassador Kuslov himself.

"I'm happy to see you, sir. I remember your father quite well. I trust his health is good, and that he is bearing up under his great responsibilities. Now, tell me, what brings you to Lisbon?"

"I had the misfortune to be playing in a chess tournament in Mannheim when the war started. All Russian, French and English players were interned. After a few months I was released, and am now trying to find a suitable, rapid way to get back to Moscow. After seeing my parents, I will join my artillery unit."

"What a terrible experience that must have been! I hope those animals didn't mistreat you?"

"It wasn't pleasant, but I survived."

"How can we help you?"

"First, I'd like to know how the war is going for us. When I came through Switzerland I was advised to try to get home by way of the Scandinavian countries. I'd appreciate your thoughts on this."

"I'll be frank with you. The Germans have had considerable success on the western front, where they have concentrated most of their power. As a result, we were able to move some distance into Poland, but there are recent signs that we may have a job hanging on to our gains. One thing is becoming clear. This war is not going to end soon. The Germans were much better armed than our intelligence services thought possible. As for getting yourself home, I agree that the Scandinavia route is probably the best to follow. So far, neutral ships in that vicinity have not been seriously molested, though that could change overnight. If you are a gambler, though, I'd say the odds are still pretty much in your favor."

"I'm going to risk it. I want to get back and do my part."

"Spoken like a true patriot."

"Do you have trouble communicating with Moscow?"

"No, our diplomatic pouches are getting through. Incidentally, if you wish to send a letter to your parents we'll be happy to send it along that way."

"That is very kind of you. I'll take advantage of your offer. Now," said Alex, getting up, "I'm certain you have more important duties to take care of. Thank you for your time, your advice, and your assistance. If I do need any other help, I'll consult your staff when I have a letter ready to send."

"Feel free to do so at any time," said the ambassador, giving him a warm handshake and a pat on the back.

The setting in Lisbon's largest chess club was in sharp contrast to the one Alex had seen in Basel. He found himself in a carpeted, well-lighted room off the mezzanine of a large, downtown hotel. There were a half-dozen substantial tables, each with four inlaid chessboards, comfortable armchairs, a large bookcase filled with an impressive collection of books on chess, and a rack holding chess journals and bulletins in a variety of languages.

He was looking at one of these when he was grabbed from behind. "Alexhine! What a surprise! How great to see you. I hadn't heard that you were free."

Alex turned to see Lupi's beaming face. "Lupi! I was hoping to find you. How have you been?"

"Oh, I'm fine. How about you? We understood you were in prison, and could be for the duration."

"I was, but luckily I managed to get away."

"What brings you to Lisbon?"

"I'm on my journey home, and was advised to go by way of Portugal and Scandinavia."

Lupi, who was still holding Alex's hand, said, "I want to hear all about everything that's happened since I last saw you. Let's go get a drink, and then you must tell me all about it."

When they entered the hotel bar, Lupi said something to one of the bartenders, then shepherded Alex to a comfortable booth. The bartender appeared promptly with a bottle, which he opened after Lupi gave it a quick look.

"Welcome to Lisbon," he said, raising his glass.

Alex tasted the wine, and exclaimed, "What a wonderful wine!"

"You like it?"

"It's the finest I've ever tasted."

"I'm happy to hear that. It's one of ours."

"Yours?"

"Yes. My family has been producing premium wines for four generations."

"Do you export it? I've never come across it anywhere."

"Oh, yes. Before the war, most of our output was going to England, with a little to Brazil. In view of the present situation, we've stopped shipments abroad, and are increasing our domestic sales somewhat, but are letting a lot of vintages continue to age, which should make then even better."

"Do you work in the business?"

"Yes. It supports the entire family. My three brothers and two sisters all work in various phases of our operations, the vineyards, the wineries, sales or distribution. I'm the baby of the family."

"Where do you fit in?"

"I'm lucky enough to be in the marketing end, which allows me enough flexibility so that I can arrange to spend quite a bit of time indulging in my various hobbies," he said, with a grin. "Chess, of course, ranks at the top."

"What are some of the others?"

"Sailing is next. In addition, I've always been interested in music, and the arts."

"It sounds as though you can lead a full, enjoyable life and still be able to approach chess seriously, without having to depend on it for a living."

"Yes, that's true."

"I guess I've been lucky that way, too, up to now, anyway. I'm not so sure about the future."

Lupi swirled the wine in his glass. "You said you are on your way home?"

"Yes, if I can get there."

The Portuguese studied him, as he sipped his wine, then said, "I suppose it's none of my business, but may I ask why?"

"Why?" Alex answered, surprised by the question. "I guess because my mother has been worried about me."

"And your father?"

"I doubt that he has had time to be concerned."

"What will you do after you get there?"

"I won't have much choice. I'll have to join my artillery unit."

"Are you anxious to see action?"

"Absolutely not. I think the whole war is an abominable thing, everyone will lose in the end."

Lupi topped their glasses while he considered that response. "How old are you, Alex?"

"Twenty-two. I had a birthday last week."

Tentative, his expression earnest, Lupi said, "I'm twenty-eight. I don't know if it qualifies me or not, but I'd like to try to talk to you as an older brother. I hope you won't think me presumptuous?"

Alex grinned. "Go right ahead. I've never had an older brother. It could be good for me."

Lupi drew a deep breath. "Okay, here goes. I don't think you should go home now."

30

"I shouldn't? Why not?"

"First of all, you said you want to relieve your mother's worries, but you won't. She's already relieved, or will be when she gets word of your escape from the Germans. Her worries will start all over again, and may be even worse, when you get into military action, wondering if you'll be killed."

Alex frowned, as though the idea had never occurred to him.

"Next, I'd like to shift the topic. Imagine that an outstanding performance takes place in some form of competition; sailing, running, boxing, football—you name it. Those lucky enough to have been present can have some memories of seeing it, but for everyone else there is probably little, other than some statistics and press reports which can't begin to capture or preserve the essence of the event." He stopped to offer Alex a cigarette and lit one for himself. Alex listened with growing interest. Where was Lupi heading?

"People worldwide with a love of chess, however, are blessed, because there are published records of countless outstanding games between the greatest players of recent centuries. And, I don't have to tell you, these can be works of art, which can be appreciated in the same way that lovers of music, painting or other arts can enjoy them."

"True," said Alex.

Lupi held his glass up, examined the color of the wine, swirled it, inhaled the aroma, then said, "Now, let's talk about you and chess. You have made it clear that your goal is to become world champion. I think you will eventually succeed, even though this unfortunate war has created a temporary obstacle."

He sipped from the glass, puffed on his cigarette, and went on, "I've been studying your games, particularly since I had the opportunity to see you in action a few times at Mannheim. Not too many have been published yet, but I am impressed with what I have seen. Some games of chess are truly outstanding. As with other artists, each player has his own style, his own concept of how to accomplish his objectives. From what I've seen, your games are beginning to show exceptional, original ideas which can bring new interest—even excitement—to the game. I am struck by the difference between your style and that of Capablanca. Without question, he is the world's strongest player at present, and will prove it when he finally corners Lasker into a match. Lasker can still beat him sometimes in tournament games, but in a long match Capa will wear him down, because of his unfailingly precise technique. His games look as though they are produced in a shop, using a lathe and grindstone, and every one comes out perfect and similar. He believes in simplification, leading to the endgames in which he has no peers."

He ground out his cigarette in the ash tray before continuing. "Your approach is just the opposite, I think you will agree. You tend to look for ways to produce positions of great complexity, in which there are many possible courses of action, and where your opponent is likely to learn, too late, which path you have chosen, and his defenses suddenly collapse. These are fascinating to study. They are done with a mallet and chisel, each unique. I believe you will continue to improve on this style, and will produce masterpieces the chess world will applaud for generations to come. Further, I think, your analyses of games are already the finest I've ever read."

He stopped to breathe deeply, and had some more wine. Alex, obviously flattered but unsure what to say, sipped his, waiting silently.

"You are twenty-two. Did you know that although he was already recognized for his talents, at twenty-two Beethoven had written none of his most wonderful works? His nine symphonies, five piano concertos, thirty-two piano sonatas, his magnificent violin concerto, and his many string quartets, just to list some. Shakespeare was past twenty-two before any of his plays appeared, and Michelangelo spent years studying with other masters before starting out on his own at about the same age. Let's suppose, instead, that these geniuses had stopped at twenty-two to fight in their nation's wars and had never come back. Think of what the world would have lost!

The images Lupi had produced caught Alex off balance. With an uncomfortable half-laugh, he protested, "Oh, come now, Lupi, you're not seriously saying that I belong in such distinguished company?"

"Not yet, but who knows? I think you have as much potential as they had at your age, but how you progress in the next ten years will give the answer."

"Unfortunately, this damned war is stopping the progress I want to make."

"Have patience, it will end. Meanwhile, there is still much you can be doing, if you keep focused on chess. I'm sure of it."

32

"Your exaggeration is flattering, of course," Alex said, after a moment of contemplation, "but I must admit that I have been having battles with my conscience ever since getting away from the Germans, about whether I should try something like what you are suggesting. It's not an easy decision."

"I'm sure it's not. I have no right to intrude, but I would hate to think that the world could possibly lose great art because I failed to speak up."

"I'm grateful for your ideas. I'll give them serious consideration, and want to discuss them with you again, some time soon."

"Great! That's all I ask." Lupi divided the last of the wine in the bottle and, instinctively, they clinked glasses again.

"Tell me about your chess club. How many members does it take to support such a nice place?"

"We have about two hundred. There are a number of well-to-do chess enthusiasts here, including the owner of the hotel, and so we are able to have good quarters and equipment."

"It certainly beats most of the clubs I've played in, even in Russia. By the way, did you have any problems getting out of Germany?"

"No, but they really shipped us out of there in a hurry. We just had time to pick up our belongings, and then were shoved into a train so crowded we had to stand for hours. That was nothing, I assume, compared to what you must have had to go through. I want to hear all about it."

"You will, but some other time. I'd better be going. There are some things I should take care of today."

"Where are you staying?"

"At a small hotel, which isn't much, but it will do until my plans crystallize."

"If you decide to stay, maybe I can help you find something better. By the way, in any case, would you consider giving an exhibition at the club sometime soon?"

"Of course. I would enjoy doing it."

The fact of the matter was that even before reaching Lisbon, Alex had almost decided against returning to Russia. Putting chess aside to fight a war didn't fit into his plans for the immediate future. Such qualms as might have been in the back of his mind faded as he listened to Lupi's unsolicited, but welcome, advice. Now, all indecision was gone. He would remain in Lisbon for the duration. He would need to earn some money, but was confident that this would not be a problem. With his contacts, Lupi should be able to help. Lupi was a man definitely worth keeping as a friend.

Alex waited two days before arranging to see him. "I've thought of nothing but your ideas, and I've finally decided to follow your advice."

Lupi was delighted. "Wonderful! I know explaining it to your family may not be easy, but I truly think you are doing the right thing."

"I hope so."

"You'll remain in Lisbon, I hope?"

"Yes, at least for the present. A lot will depend on how long the war lasts."

"Good. Now what can I do to help? You did say you needed a place to live? What do you have in mind?"

"Something very simple, but conveniently located, if possible."

Lupi thought a moment. "It happens there is a small apartment not far from here which I believe is available. A fellow I know just moved out of it last week. I've never been in it, but he seemed quite satisfied. I can get the address in a few minutes if you want to look at it today."

"Of course. I'd like to see it before someone else takes it."

Too narrow for vehicles, the path led uphill past vine-covered, staggered walls, behind which houses of assorted sizes, shapes and colors elbowed one another. A pair of small birds took off from the compact garden thick with flowering shrubs when Alex opened the gate. He was about to knock on the door when a girl holding a pair of pruning shears came from around the side of the house.

"Can I help you?" she said, eyeing this tall well-dressed stranger.

"I hope so. I am told there may be an apartment here for rent."

"Just a moment, I'll get my mother."

Not bad, he thought, watching the slender, dark-eyed girl, who looked to be about eighteen, go through the door, her long, black hair swinging from side to side.

Except for her eyes, which inspected him sharply, the stocky woman with bobbed, gray-streaked hair who appeared bore little resemblance to her daughter. "You are looking for an apartment?"

"Yes," he said, removing his hat, "my name is Alexander Alekhine. I have just arrived here and am hoping to enroll in some courses at the university, so I am looking for a small, quiet place."

"I do have one vacancy. Another student occupied it until last week. I'll show you."

The girl watched with interest as Alex followed her mother around the side of the house.

The apartment, with its own outside entrance, had been carved from the large house. It consisted of a single room, furnished with bed, chest of drawers, bookcase, table with three chairs, plus private bath and a small alcove equipped for simple kitchen functions. The rent being less than he had anticipated, the apartment suited Alex and he said he would take it.

It was actually more rent than she had charged the previous tenant, but only slightly. She didn't want to scare off such a promising-looking young man with exceptionally nice manners, even though he appeared more prosperous than the former occupant. "I am Maria Pereira," she said, handing Alex a receipt for the deposit he had paid, after following her into her living room, "and this is Rosa, my youngest daughter. The other two are married and live elsewhere in Lisbon. Rosa is a violinist and is studying at the conservatory."

"It's a pleasure" he said, giving a formal nod—almost a bow—to each of them, a shy smile on his face.

"May I ask where you are from?" the mother asked.

"I am from Russia."

"Really? I'm surprised they don't have you in the army."

"They do. I have a commission in the intelligence service, and have been given a deferment to improve my knowledge of languages."

"You speak Portuguese quite well."

"Thank you, but I have studied it only a little, so far."

When Alex had gone, after arranging to move in the following day, Maria smiled at her daughter, who blushed.

Dearest Mother,
It seems an eternity since I left for Mannheim, in spite of your reservations. I should have followed your advice. I regret the worry I know I have caused you, and I can't tell you how grateful I am for your arranging with Grandfather to get me out of Germany. I won't tell you about the

time I spent there, because I just want to wipe it out of my mind.

I hate to tell you, but I have had more incredibly bad luck. I had gone to inquire about ship schedules to Norway—the route Grandfather recommended—and as I was crossing a street, a horse, apparently frightened by an automobile, bolted and kicked me, breaking my ankle. The doctor says I won't be able to travel for at least a couple of months.

Fortunately, I have enough money (I received the first-prize money at Mannheim, and was given more as a result of the arrangements Grandfather made with a bank in Basel) so don't worry.

I have been able to find a comfortable place to stay and, with practice, am getting used to crutches.

I'll spend the time here studying, so it won't be a total waste. I'm sorry that it will be longer before I get to see you, and before I can join my army unit—but at least—it will be better than the time in Germany, so don't worry.

All my love,

Alex

He used sealing wax, impressed with the signet ring he always wore, to seal the letter, donned his jacket and hat, and went striding down the hill on his way to leave the letter at the Russian Embassy. That responsibility out of the way, he spent the next five hours, as was already his custom, at the chess club. He played occasional games, but concentrated most of his time to studying the books in its collection.

"Will you be ready to give an exhibition soon?" Lupi asked, the next time they met.

"Whenever you'd like. I've been thinking about it, and have a suggestion to offer. Instead of the usual simultaneous, I'd like to try playing four blindfold games at once. I've never tried doing more than one at a time, and want to see if I can. What do you think?"

"I think that's a sensational idea! I'll take it up at the meeting of the club's board of governors."

The board shared his enthusiasm and scheduled the performance for the following week. The fee they guaranteed was enough to take care of Alex's rent for a couple of months.

When he was only ten years old, Alex had discovered that he could play a game of chess without seeing the board. He and a classmate with similar ability would stealthily pass each other notes, during class, bearing their moves. He practiced further, lying in bed at night and playing over games by memory. This talent was honed through the many games he had played during internment. The idea to try several games at once came to him from one of the books at the Lisbon club, which had an account of twenty-two simultaneous blindfold games played by the American master, Harry Nelson Pillsbury. Who knows? Perhaps he could break that record some day.

❖ ❖ ❖

A large audience was on hand on a Friday evening when he sat down in an upholstered armchair facing a high window. A small table beside him held containers of water, coffee and wine, as well as an ash tray and three packs of cigarettes. Outwardly he showed no signs of uneasiness but, for once, he was aware of the perspiration under his armpits.

His opponents sat on one side of two tables a dozen feet behind him. At the ends of each table large demonstration boards had been set up so that the spectators could watch the progress of the games. Those lucky enough to arrive early had seats in a double row of chairs. The rest of the audience had to stand behind them. Four of Lisbon's strongest chess players—including Lupi, the current national champion—furnished Alex's opposition.

"We can start whenever you are ready," the director of the event told Alex, after he had explained the procedure to the assemblage.

"Fine," said Alex, who would be playing White on the first and third boards, "pawn to King Four on Board One."

Another official moved the pawn to the appropriate square on the first board, and announced the opponent's response. Alex, as well as the official, called out the moves loudly enough to be heard clearly throughout the room.

As the games progressed Alex responded to each adversary's move before going to the next game. Once play was under way he lost all sense of nervousness, his concentration complete. A pack of cigarettes and five cups of coffee later, with only one game still in progress, he paused long enough to down a half-glass of wine, then announced, "Mate in three."

His opponent studied his board for a moment, nodded, turned down his King, and conceded, "Correct, I resign."

Alex drained the last of the glass of wine as he was rising to turn and acknowledge the enthusiastic response from the audience. He had lost one game, drawn one, and won two, including the game against Lupi. Much as he always hated to lose any game, he was not too dissatisfied with the results of his first venture into this kind of competition.

Five

The constantly shifting collage of positions from those four games, of the warm audience response, and of Lupi's earnest face made sleep impossible for hours. At four o'clock, he succeeded in knocking himself out by gulping a large glass of brandy...

> *The internees are rejoicing because their guards have just brought them several fine chess sets and boards. Their games are hardly under way when his father, wearing the uniform of a German general, comes in and shouts, "This is verboten!" and, with a single stroke of his saber, sweeps the pieces off all of the boards. Furious, Alex jumps to his feet to protest but, when his father spits in his face and strides over to where his mother is laughing with delight, he just stands there weeping, a mixture of tears and saliva running down his cheeks.*

Alex startled awake from his nightmare, sweating profusely and completely drained. Already past noon, he staggered to the sink, stuck his head under the faucet and let the cold water stream over him for a minute. He drank three glasses of water, added water to the coffee pot, and sat on the edge of the bed to wait for it to boil. After two cups of the astringent, black brew, plus a slice of bread with jam, he felt restored enough to shave and dress, with the thought of going to the chess club, However, the prospect of subjecting himself to a walk of even that short distance had little appeal, and he spent the rest of the day in his room studying various king and pawn endgame positions. After it grew dark, he did go out to a restaurant for his only meal of the day, with which he limited himself to a single glass of red wine. While he lingered over a cigarette, he considered options available for the evening, but in the end ignored the festive Saturday night crowds filling the streets, paid his bill, and decided to return home and get a good night's sleep.

A visit to the chess club in mind, Alex encountered Maria and Rosa Pereira leaving their home early Sunday afternoon.

"Good afternoon," he said, tipping his hat.

"Mr. Alekhine," said the mother, "how nice to see you. Have you gotten settled yet?"

"Yes, very comfortably, thank you. I am pleased with the quarters. This is certainly a fine afternoon, isn't it?"

"Indeed. It's much too nice to ignore, so Rosa and I have decided to walk in the park at the top of the hill. Have you seen it?"

"No, I wasn't aware of one."

"If you are free would you care to join us?"

Chess had much more appeal, but some dividends might eventually come from maintaining a good relationship with this pair. He smiled, "I would welcome the privilege. I had no particular plans except to enjoy the weather."

He followed them as they walked single file up the winding path to the crest, where the hill suddenly flattened into a surprisingly spacious, informally-planted park, surrounded by a low, stone wall. The view wherever he looked was spectacular. In three directions the city spread as far as one could see. In the fourth, looking straight down over the wall, he saw the spray from waves beating against sharp rocks a hundred feet below.

Both women pointed out features of interest, and answered his many questions about the area. After completing the circuit within the wall, they sat on a bench.

"Rosa has been working extra hard lately," said her mother. "She is getting ready for a recital at the conservatory two weeks from today."

"What are you playing?" Alex asked the girl.

"The Tchaikovsky Concerto."

"Oh, that's my favorite," he said. There was no point in adding that it was the only one he knew of.

"You enjoy music?" asked Maria.

"I love it, particularly the music of Russia. While I've never learned to play an instrument—my own studies are too time-consuming—I try to listen to it whenever I get the chance."

Maria gave her daughter a quick glance, then said, "Would you be interested in attending a concert this Thursday evening? A string quartet will be playing. Doesn't the program include some Russian music, Rosa?"

"Yes, they are doing some Borodin and Moussorgsky."

"If you'd care to hear it, Rosa has tickets. I'm not very interested in chamber music. I prefer vocal works."

"I'd enjoy it very much, but I wouldn't want to keep you from attending."

"I won't mind at all, I assure you. You'd really be doing me a favor."

"In that case," he said, looking at Rosa, "if you are willing to put up with my company I shall look forward to enjoying the music in your company."

"I'll be happy to have you instead of Mother. She really doesn't care for such programs," she said, coloring slightly.

Before going to the chess club the next day, Alex visited the public library, where he spent some time with books on Russian composers, accumulating enough information about the works of several, along with various anecdotes about their lives, to give the impression of some familiarity with the subject. It never hurt to be prepared.

The extent of Alex's knowledge of music was not especially on Rosa's mind as they left for the concert. There was something intriguing about him that aroused her curiosity the first time she had seen him. Various young men, including both fellow students and faculty members, had shown interest in her, but she had kept her distance, concentrating on preparing for the career she planned. This evening, though, her thoughts were straying from that objective.

As for Alex, he found this serious girl attractive, and he looked forward to a pleasant evening with the possibility of others to follow. Wherever they might lead, though, they would never be allowed to divert him from his own goal. Nothing had, not even imprisonment. Nothing ever would.

"How long have you been playing the violin?" he asked.

"I started when I was six."

"Really? Have you been studying it continuously since then?"

"Yes, eleven years."

"You must be very accomplished."

"I'd better be. I plan to have a professional career with it."

"Teaching?"

"Some of that will probably be necessary. Self-supporting concert careers are hard to achieve, particularly for women, but I hope to be good enough to do it."

"How about the rest of your family? Do they support your career plans?"

His interest pleased her. "It all goes back to my father. He was the one who bought my first violin, an undersized one, and taught me how to play." Her face turned sober. "He died three years ago, and I still miss him terribly. He was a very fine cellist, playing with amateur groups whenever he had the chance. He gave me his love for music. After teaching me a few months he arranged for me to perform at the conservatory, after which they agreed to accept me as a student." Her smile returned as she added, "I was their youngest student for the next few years."

"That's impressive. You must have very exceptional talent," he said.

"That's what my father told me. Before he died he set up a trust fund for me to insure that I could continue my studies and try for a concert career."

"What about your sisters?"

"I was the baby of the family. One of them was eight and the other seven when I was born."

"Do they share your interest in music?"

"They both play the piano well enough for their own entertainment, but their main interests are their families and the business."

"Business?"

"My father owned a ship's chandlery, and both sisters married men who worked for him. They, along with mother, inherited the business, and their husbands run it."

"I assume your mother approves of your career plans?"

"Yes, although I believe that was something which she left entirely for Father and me to decide. She has her own interests, and looks after the property. Our house was larger than necessary for just the two of us, so she had parts of it converted into three small apartments, which gives her income to supplement what she gets from the business."

42

Strolling home, after the concert and a stop for refreshments, she said, "All we've talked about is me and my career. Tell me something about yourself."

"There's not much to tell. I've had a comfortable existence, and spent most of my time studying. Having a commission in the reserves, I expected to be called to active duty when the war started, but the higher-ups decided it was more important that I broaden my language capabilities. To be truthful, I'm quite happy with their decision. I'd rather be here doing this than at the front. I'll go when called, but I'm not in a hurry to have a leg blown off."

"I don't blame you. Getting back to languages, which ones do you speak?"

"I can handle French, German, and English without any problems, and Spanish reasonably well. As you can tell, my Portuguese needs a lot of work."

"No it doesn't. You speak it beautifully. I wish I could do as well with foreign languages. If I'm to concertize, I'll be traveling a lot and will need to get along in other countries."

"Which ones have you studied?"

"I've concentrated on French and English, but still don't speak either well enough. Because of our history, everyone here can speak Spanish, but most of us refuse to use it when speaking to someone from Spain." She laughed. "We make them use our language. It's a matter of pride."

"If you have the time, and would like to, I'd be glad to work with you on your English and French."

Her eyes glowed with delight. "Would you? I'd love it."

"Just say when."

She thought it over. "Even though I won't have much free time until after my concert, I think a break from practicing might be a good idea. Could we do it next Thursday evening?"

"Fine. My schedule is flexible."

When they reached her front door, he said, "Thank you for the nicest evening I've had in a long time."

"Thank you. It's been a wonderful change for me, too, and I'm really looking forward to next Thursday." With that, she reached up, pulled his head down, kissed his cheek, then dashed into the house.

Walking around to his own front door, Alex grinned. It had been a pleasant evening for him. He found this girl quite a change from the shallow daughters of his parents' friends.

The two bulging string bags Maria Pereira was carrying as she trudged up the winding path slowed her progress, and Alex caught up with her on his way home.

"Let me have one of those," he said.

"Gladly," she said, pausing to catch her breath. "I went overboard in my shopping today."

"I'm happy I found you. I've been wanting to thank you for the opportunity to hear that concert the other evening. It was very enjoyable."

"I'm glad. Rosa told me she enjoyed the evening, too."

"She's very good company. You have an exceptional daughter."

"Thanks. She told me of your offer to help her with her language studies. That's very nice of you."

"Not at all. I know how helpful practice can be."

They entered the house and he followed her into the kitchen, where they deposited the bags.

"I'm going to make coffee to have with some sweet rolls I bought. Would you care to have some? That is, if you don't mind the company of an old woman."

Apparently puzzled, Alex looked quizzically from side to side. "I didn't realize there was someone else here."

She laughed. "You flatterer! It's a good thing you aren't a few years older."

Rosa arrived for her ten o'clock lesson the following Wednesday only to learn that her teacher had an emergency at home and had left word for her to return at three that afternoon. The unexpected free time gave her an opportunity to do some preparing for her Thursday evening date. She wanted to get some cologne and, though she knew her mother would disapprove, some rouge.

On her way, she stopped off at home to leave her violin. As she walked through the hall past the half-open door to her mother's bedroom she thought she heard a slight moan. Stepping back, she looked in. Their naked bodies glued together, her mother straddled Alex.

Zelda, the forty-five-year-old housekeeper who had relieved the fifteen-year-old Alex of his virginity, had been an accomplished teacher. Subsequent sexual research during the next few years with females of his own generation, while pleasant, led him to the conclusion that there was a lot to be said for experience. He confirmed this to his satisfaction during a number of afternoons spent in the bedrooms of some of his mother's lifelong friends. Further encounters also taught him that many mature women were receptive—even grateful—when he made appropriate overtures. Maria Pereira was no exception.

Wrapped in a robe, much of the color was gone from her face when she returned to the bedroom. She had gone to investigate the sound of the front door slamming. A note was in her hand. "Trouble. Rosa saw us."

"Are you sure?" he said, sitting up abruptly.
"I found this on the hall table."

> I shall never return to this house! I'll send for the rest of
> my things. How could you do this to me?

"She didn't bother to sign it."
"What could she do? Where will she go?"
"She's probably gone to one of her sisters. I looked in her room. A suitcase and some of her clothes are gone, as well as her violin and all her music."
"She can't mean it about never coming back, can she? Can she get by on her own?"
Distressed, beginning to tremble, Maria shook her head. "I'm not sure. She's a stubborn, determined girl. She has some money her father left her, she earns a little more teaching a few children, and her conservatory expenses are paid up for the year. If her performance Sunday is successful, she may be able to earn more. Everyone says she is really a talented violinist."
"What will you do?"
She shrugged in frustration. "I'm not sure. Maybe I'll give her a few days to cool off before I try to get in touch with her, unless one of her sisters contacts me."

45

"I am truly sorry about this. If there is any way I can help...?"

She stared at him. "Just don't leave me at this point. There is no one else I can talk to."

"Of course I won't." He rose from the bed and put his arms around her. She clutched him, shuddering. After an interval, she calmed enough to look up, tears and a wan smile on her face. "I'm depending on you. I couldn't bear to be totally alone."

"You won't be," he said, then kissed her softly. She responded gently, then with urgency, as she pushed him back against the bed.

Six

Even chess players have to eat. The additional funds Alex found waiting at the Lisbon bank added to what he brought with him, plus his fee for the exhibition, were enough to carry him for several months, and still leave enough to get himself home, should he change his plans. If he wanted wine with his meals, though, and possibly an occasional night out, some extra money was needed. He might earn some through chess, but not much as long as he stayed in Portugal. He took his problem to Lupi.

"What kind of work are you looking for?"

"I'm not sure, except that it must be only part-time. I've never had to work, but I'd think my knowledge of languages should be useful to someone."

"I'd think so. Let me talk to a few people."

The next time they met, Lupi had good news. "There's this monthly magazine which concentrates on social and political subjects. The publisher is a friend of mine. He says he needs more help, and will be glad to pay you to translate articles from foreign sources. In addition, the local manager of one of the news wire services said for you to come in to talk about possibly doing something similar with dispatches from other countries."

"Those sound great. Thank you, Lupi. I owe a lot to you."

Lupi laughed. "Not really. Having talked you into not getting killed, I should at least keep you from dying of malnutrition."

❖ ❖ ❖

The two jobs made an ideal combination. Alex handled the wire service duties at its offices in an hour or two in the mornings. The work for the magazine he did at home at his own convenience. This allowed at least six hours a day for chess. He played in occasional Portuguese tournaments, gave a few exhibitions around the country, explored new theories and concepts with Lupi, and devoured all of the chess literature he could get his hands on

He also spent most of his nights with Maria, whose need for him was desperate, particularly after her two older daughters had let her know of their own anger and disgust. Her only family contacts were through her sons-in-law. Though they kept their own views from their wives, secretly they were both rather amused at the whole episode. Of course, those weren't the only secrets concerning sex they kept from their wives. Iberian men would be men. Maria did not dare attend Rosa's important concert. The one Lisbon paper which covered the event gave it laudatory review. She put three copies of it in her dresser after reading it through tears. The temptation to beg forgiveness from her three children was great, but she held back. Months passed, as the standoff in the Pereira family continued.

Alex didn't care who won the war. He just wanted it to end. The wire service reports kept him abreast of what was happening on the fronts. As trench warfare took over, prospects for an early end shrank. His frustration grew. Foreign commentaries which he translated for the magazine only served to increase his gloom week by week. His chances for any significant international chess competition seemed ever more remote.

"I don't know how much longer I can wait for this damn war to end! I'm tempted to try to get to the United States or to South America."

"Don't even think about it," Lupi warned. "I read every day how the German subs are covering the Atlantic, and they no longer hesitate to sink neutral ships."

"Don't tell me. I see the dispatches even before the papers get them."

"All you can do is have patience."

His eyes blazing, he slammed down his glass, spilling a few drops. "Goddamnit! I've been patient for two years!"

"I know how hard it is, Alex, but in life, just as in chess, sometimes patience is the only thing."

"Don't preach to me!" Alex snapped, getting up and stomping away.

He concentrated on events in the west, where the outcome of the conflict would be determined. Even so, he could not ignore accounts of the chain of Russian military reverses month after month. Evidence of internal unrest began to seep through censorship. Official voices promptly dismissed as lies all stories of revolutionary activity in his homeland, but these continued to multiply.

Nevertheless, Alex could not visualize any threat to his parents, or disruption of the Russian lifestyle he had known. He had only disbelief of the first hints that the tsar and his family had been seized, but when no denials followed, an icy chill went through him. Suddenly, he realized that the world in which he had been raised could be coming to an end.

"What kind of wine?" Alex asked, as he adjusted his tie. In the mirror he could see where Maria still lay.

"Why don't you bring both a red and a white?"

"All right. I should be back by five-thirty." He put on his jacket, blew her a kiss, and left the room without a hint that he expected this was the last time she would ever see him.

"It isn't what I planned, but now I don't have a choice. I have to be there if they need help."

"I understand. The best of luck, Alex. I hope we'll meet again soon under happier circumstances," Lupi said, embracing him.

"Thanks again, for everything," said Alex. "No one ever had a better friend."

It was the *Crown of Stockholm*, a small, rusty freighter, bound for its home port of Göteborg. The bunk took up most of his cabin. He and two Swedish businessmen were the only passengers. They had their meals with the captain, a gloomy graybeard named Larsen, and First Officer Johannsen. Neither ever smiled. They seldom spoke, and the captain's responses to questions were laconic. He did tell them that he had made five round-trips from various Scandinavian ports to destinations in Portugal and Spain since the outbreak of war. They had been stopped and boarded by the Germans for questioning a number of times, but had always been allowed to proceed.

They didn't linger at the table after meals. Alex either spent time on his bunk with his pocket chess set or on deck smoking, as he wondered what lay ahead for him, including what might happen to him if the ship were stopped and boarded.

Relieved, he stood at the rail looking at the lights on the Göteborg docks when they dropped anchor in the harbor for the night. The trip had been uneventful.

It's a good thing he brought two bottles. The first one is almost empty, and there's no telling how long he'll need to wait in the frigid darkness, and the wind is picking up. That lying bitch!

"My last night here for God knows how many months."

"I know, Olaf, but I can't help it. Fredrika and the baby are both sick in bed, and Ragnar is working until midnight. I just have to be there until he gets home."

He knows she is lying, and proves it that afternoon when he watches Ragnar leave for work. Fredrika, carrying the baby, has come outside with him, and they stand there awhile, talking and laughing. After he kisses them and leaves, she puts the baby in the stroller and they disappear down the street.

His vigil pays off shortly after eleven o'clock. He hears a man's voice and her shrieking laugh. When the door opens and the light goes on, the tall, burly figure with her is instantly recognizable. Erik! Of all people! There's no mistaking him. He slings the empty bottle into the bushes, opens the other. The gulp he takes is so large it makes him choke and cough, but his eyes never leave the house across the street. In a short time, a light appears upstairs and the one downstairs goes off. There are moving shadows on the shade of the bedroom window, then that room also becomes dark. Half-an-hour later, Olaf leaves, walking slowly, the shape of a plan beginning to evolve in his mind.

On the voyage south, Olaf, a short, wiry seaman on the *Crown of Stockholm*, carries out his duties well enough that even the vicious second mate, Erik, who is responsible for discipline among the crew finds few opportunities to criticize him. Off-duty, Olaf plays cards, as usual, with fellow crew members. Otherwise, he is somewhat quieter than usual, but no one notices.

At Lisbon, the final stop on the return trip, he buys a pistol which he is able to hide in his sea bag without anyone noticing.

He waits for the right moment as, late at night, they draw close to the Göteborg docks and drop anchor.

Erik is only fifteen feet in front of Olaf when he aims the pistol. Trying to keep his hand steady, he fires. There is a cry.

Erik whirled around. A dark figure was slipping over the rail. There was a splash, then the sound of someone swimming away. He turned back to where he could see the dark stain growing on the back of Alex's jacket, as his grip on the rail relaxed and he began sliding down.

"What was that?" the first mate shouted from the bridge.

"Man shot!" Erik cried.

"Get Johannsen! I'll get the captain."

First Officer Johannsen handled medical emergencies aboard the ship. Grabbing his bag of supplies he hurries after Erik to where Alex lay unconscious.

Captain Larsen wasn't far behind. "Is he alive?"

"Yes," the first officer said. Helped by Erik, he had stripped Alex to the waist. "It's a nasty wound. He's bleeding a lot."

Larson rushed to the radio room. "Get in touch with the harbor master. Tell him a man has been shot and there's an urgent need for medical help."

"Does anyone know what happened?" he asked, when he returned where Johannsen was working to stop the bleeding.

"I was right there," said Erik. "I even felt the shot go past me. I turned and saw someone go over the rail and heard a splash."

"No idea who it was?"

"No, sir. It was too dark."

Larsen frowned. "Could he have been shooting at you?"

Erik shrugged. "Could be."

The captain went back to the radio operator. "Did you get them?"

"Yes, sir. They are sending help."

"Contact them again to be on the lookout for anyone swimming ashore."

Half-an-hour later, two launches arrived, one carrying a doctor, harbor police in the other.

"I've stopped most of the bleeding," Johannsen told the doctor, "but he's lost a lot of blood."

"We've got to get him to the hospital right away," the doctor said, after a brief examination. "That bullet needs to come out."

As soon as Alex had been taken off the ship, the police conferred with Larsen. "Any idea who did this, Captain?"

"No, but I think we'll know, as soon as we do a roll call. It had to be someone already on board."

It didn't take long to learn that one member of the crew was missing—Olaf.

"It's probably not much consolation to you," said the police officer, who had accompanied the doctor into the room, "but at least you know that you weren't the intended target. The fellow just couldn't shoot straight, and you were unlucky enough to be there."

Alex grimaced. "My luck hasn't been very good for quite awhile, but I guess I can be thankful for just being alive."

"That's very true," the doctor told the policeman. "He developed blood poisoning, which easily could have been fatal. It was touch and go for about ten days. If it had taken another hour to get him to the hospital, I doubt that he would have made it. He was lucky that the bullet didn't penetrate the lung, and there shouldn't be much permanent muscle damage."

"Where were you going?" asked the officer.

"I'm on my way to Moscow."

The officer's face grew grave. "From the rumors I hear, Russia's one place I'd avoid right now, unless my business there was really urgent."

"I'm afraid that it is, and I've already lost a couple of weeks here."

"We'll probably be releasing you in a couple of days," the doctor told Alex, "but don't even think about doing any traveling for at least two more weeks, and I want to examine you before you do leave. That's an order."

Alex raised his hand in a salute. To the officer he said, "This guy's a tyrant. No one here dares breathe unless he gives permission."

A week later, Alex resumed his trip to Moscow without bothering to consult anyone.

52

Seven

It was a long, depressing walk. Farms devoid of crops, animals a rare sight. The few people he saw, usually elderly, viewed him with suspicion, and hurried to avoid contact. The closer he got to his destination, the greater the sense of dismay gripping him. It was hard to comprehend the smashed walls, iron gates off their hinges, and scorched debris around stone chimneys, all that remained of mansions. The interiors of many of them had been familiar to him. At the crest of the hill he found the house he had left.

Aghast, he stood in the road for a long minute before passing through the wreckage of the once-proud gateway. He stepped cautiously around heaps of rubble, bricks, burnt timbers, fragments of glass, until he found himself within the shell of what remained. A sickening stench of the fire was overwhelming. Evidence of vandalism was everywhere. He looked around, awed by the extent of the destruction, and not really able to measure it. Then, it dawned on him that the north wing, where his room had been, had completely vanished, taking with it his complete chess library, together with the records of every tournament and correspondence game he had ever played. Also gone were all of his trophies. Like a saber, that realization ripped through his belly, and he began to roar, to bellow, to scream obscenities, then to sob uncontrollably.

Then there were arms around him. Another tear-stained face pressed against his. "Mr. Alex! Mr. Alex! At last!"

"Zelda!" He clung to her, shuddering. When he could breathe again, he said, "What happened? Where is Mother?"

"Come," she said, leading him out of the wreckage back to a hut near the remains of what had been the carriage house. Somehow it had been spared. With nowhere else to go it was now her refuge.

"It was terrible!" she said, after they were seated on boxes. "They came in the middle of the night, last week."

"Who? Who came?"

"A mob, that's all I know. Men with guns, with axes, with pitchforks. They knocked down the gate and rushed the house. Your father came to the top of the stairs with his pistols and shot two of them. Then he was hit and fell down the stairs. Your mother ran to him, but they pulled them apart, then killed both of them. I came in from the other wing with other servants just in time to see it. It was horrible!"

Through her tears and trembling she struggled on. "Their leader told us we were now free from slavery, but to get out at once as they were going to burn down the house. Before they did, though, they tore the place apart, looting, stealing everything they could carry. What they couldn't move or didn't want they crushed with axes. Then they lit the fires and left. Oh, Mr. Alex, I can't tell you how awful it was!" The tears gushed as she finished.

"And I wasn't here to help!" he blurted, guilt mixed with grief.

"You could do nothing against that mob. They would have killed you, too. Thank God, you are still alive!"

He stumbled on toward the distant center of the city, his mind out of control. A mob of emotions—rage, grief, fear, guilt—overran any coherent thought that popped up. Nausea gripped him. Coming to a stone wall, he pressed his hands against it, leaning forward, as though to push away this nightmare. He retched. There was nothing in him except bile, but the spasms seemed to eject the emotions as well, and he found himself aware only of his total isolation. A sense of complete impotence enveloped him.

Late afternoon. Aimless wanderings eventually brought him into the presence of others, mostly men. A few seemed to be on their way to specific destinations, but most just stood around, some alone, others in clumps, conversing carefully in low, dispirited voices. Along each block men wearing red armbands, pistols fastened at their belts, scrutinized each passerby. Some they would stop to examine identification papers. Once or twice Alex thought he was about to be questioned.

He had paused at a corner, next to two better-dressed men, when

54

an armed man on horseback passed. His steed, perhaps at his urging, stepped in a puddle of muddy water, splashing the three of them.

"The bloody bastard!" one of them exploded in English, scowling at the horseman, who glanced back with an amused smirk.

"Blast him! He did it on purpose!" the other raged.

Even Alex was aroused from his stupor. "He wouldn't have dared do that before the war."

Surprised, one of them turned to him, saying, "My word! Don't tell me you're English, too?"

"No, I'm Russian."

"Then you must have studied at Cambridge."

"No, but my tutor did."

A quick glance passed between the foreigners, then one said, "You are the first English-speaking Russian we've found. We can't let you get away. Do you have to be anywhere in the next hour?"

"No, I'm not going anywhere."

"Then we'd like you to join us. We're on our way to a place we've found where one can get a drink and almost acceptable food, unless you can guide us to a better meal."

"No, I know nothing. I've just returned after several years out of the country."

"That settles it," said the taller of the two, a man in this early thirties. "I'm Roger Sloane, from Manchester and," pointing to his chunky, older companion, "this blasted Welshman with me is Fred Evans."

"I am Alexander Alekhine," he said, shaking hands with each of them. "I'll be glad to accompany you. I haven't eaten today, and I really need a drink, a strong one."

"You do look as though you could use a couple," said Sloane, after an appraising glance.

Seated at a small table, a few minutes later, Evans poured vodka into three small glasses, raised his and said, "To better days."

"Amen," said Sloane.

"A fitting thought. Nothing could possibly be worse than today," Alex responded, and gulped the contents of his glass.

The others also tossed theirs off. Evans promptly refilled the glasses.

Sloane looked at Alex. "You do seem stressed. Would it help you to talk about it? Not that we want to pry."

He seldom revealed personal matters, even to close friends, but Alex welcomed the chance to unburden himself. "In a nutshell, I reached Moscow just today, only to find that my parents had been murdered last week and our home vandalized and burned." He emptied his glass, then shuddered, as he covered his face with both hands.

"Good God!" said Evans, astonished.

"Christ!" breathed Sloane.

The two stared at each other, then watched Alex reach for the bottle and pour himself a third drink, which he downed immediately.

"Maybe we'd better have something to eat," said Evans.

❖ ❖ ❖

The door Sloane unlocked two hours later let them enter a small, windowless room. Its crude furnishings, revealed after Evans lit a smoky, oil lamp, consisted of a bed, a small table holding a pitcher and wash basin, and a trunk on which a few articles of clothing were resting.

"You can sleep here tonight," Sloane said. "I'll bunk with Fred. His room is just down the block. Get some rest and we'll look in on you tomorrow."

Alex muttered his thanks and, as soon as they were gone, tossed his jacket on the trunk and, without taking off his shoes, was out like a light as soon as he hit the bed.

Evans and Sloane crossed the street to a door directly opposite the one they had just closed. Evans rapped twice quickly, once more after a pause, then gave two more taps.

"What's up?" asked the bearded man who opened the door a crack, then wide enough to allow them to slip in.

"Maybe something of interest," Evans said.

The four roughly dressed men sat around a table holding glasses, a bottle, and some scattered papers.

"What's so interesting"? asked the bearded man, obviously the group's spokesman.

"We may have a new recruit."

"Tell us."

"A young fellow named Alekhine. Says his father was president of

56

the duma before the war. The guy claims he's been out of the country since July of 1914 and just got back and found that his parents had been killed and their home gutted. If he's telling the truth, he might want to enlist. He'd certainly have reason to be bitter."

"If he is an Alekhine, he probably is telling the truth," the other said, after a pause. "I remember that the head of the duma for awhile was named Alekhine. Why was he out of the country?"

"He says he was in Germany playing in a chess tournament when the war started, and was interned for awhile. When he was released he decided the smart thing was to stay away for the duration. Says he worked as a translator and continued language studies."

"Where?"

"Portugal. Claims to speak a half-dozen languages. I'll say this, he speaks English without a trace of an accent."

"That sounds like the kind of education his family would have given—what's that racket outside?"

Sloane darted to the window and peered through a crack in the curtain. "There's a bunch of men across the street, two on horseback—and here comes a patrol wagon. Cripes! They're breaking down the door over there!"

"Quick, douse the light!" said the bearded man, rushing to see.

Evans shook his head, appalled. "That poor slob!"

Drained and drunk as he was, the crash of the door splintering first seemed part of a dream. The illusion ended abruptly when he was yanked to his feet, then slammed against the wall. Dazed and terrified, he watched men turn over his bed and rip open the thin pad which had served as his mattress. Finding nothing, they swept everything off the trunk. Its lock was shattered by a blow from a rifle butt, the lid was opened and the contents of the trunk exposed.

Minutes later, he found himself inside the patrol wagon along with the trunk and two guards. They were laughing, as the wagon began moving, pleased with the success of the raid. Nausea soon overwhelmed Alex as they swayed and bumped. He vomited, spraying the shoes of both men, whose chortles turned to curses, as their enclosure began to stink. The tortuous journey finally ended. Supported on each side by the disgruntled pair, he stumbled along a dimly-lighted, musty corridor to a small room equipped with a table and two chairs. The guards removed his chains before leaving him. He collapsed in a chair, cradled his head in his arms on the table, and waited.

Hours later, he raised his head as he heard a key in the door. A slender man entered and seated himself across from him. An armed guard stood at the door, impassive. The face Alex stared at was long, narrow, and swarthy. Above a bushy mustache he saw a twisted nose and cold, cobra eyes.

His visitor studied him, while packing tobacco into a large, curved pipe. After lighting it to his satisfaction and dropping the match on the floor, he asked in a flat, unemotional voice, "Your name?"

Alex struggled to find this voice. "Please, could I have some water?"

The man nodded to the guard, who returned a moment later with a grimy, half-full glass.

Alex clutched it with both hands, gulped its contents gratefully and, maintaining his grip to restrain their trembling, said, "I am Alexander Alekhine."

Where do you live?"

"At the moment I have no home. I was wounded on the eastern front, and was just released from an Austrian hospital. I reached Moscow yesterday and found that my parents had been killed and our home destroyed."

"Indeed? Who was your father?"

"Victor Alekhine."

A slight smile, the first sign of any expression, appeared on his questioner's face. "Then what did you do?"

Alex shook his head. "It's not too clear. I walked a long time, maybe hours. I met two men. We had drinks and food. I guess I drank too much. They must have felt sorry for me and took me to a room where there was a bed. They said they'd come back in the morning. The next thing I knew, I was being brought here."

"These friends of yours? What are their names?"

"They weren't friends. I'd never seen them before."

"Why did they pick you up?"

"I guess it was because they were speaking English, and were glad to find someone who spoke their language."

"Who were they?" The questions came in rapid fire.

"Their names were Evans and Sloane. Uh, Fred Evans and Roger Sloane."

"What were they doing here?"

"Let me think—yes, they said they were free-lance journalists getting material for a book about what's happening here."

"And you believed them?"

"I had no reason not to. Besides, I wasn't paying too much attention. I already had more on my mind than I could handle."

His interrogator stared at him without blinking, puffing on his pipe, then stood up and said, "Lock him up."

Eight

The dank, cramped cell, with its insufferable stink, was dark, dirty, degrading. Once in awhile he would stir himself and pace furiously, but most of the time he just sat on his bunk, stymied, totally dejected. Except to bring his meals—miserable slop, which he barely touched—the guards ignored him. Occupants of the adjoining cells, busy contending with their own devils, did not disturb him. It was the fourth day before they came for him.

The courtroom was sparingly furnished. Facing him were three, grim-faced men sitting at a long table. To his left two men sat at a smaller one. One guard stood at the only door and two other armed men occupied the only other chairs in the room.

After shuffling some papers, one of the men at the long table said, "Next."

The cold-eyed man who had questioned him selected some papers from the side table and handed three sheets to each of the trio. The other man at the smaller table prepared to take notes.

"The People versus Alexander Alekhine," the presiding judge read aloud. "Comrade Prosecutor, what is the charge?"

"Members of the People's Court, the defendant, Alexander Alekhine, is charged with the possession of illegal weapons and subversive, counterrevolutionary materials, with the objective of destroying the lawful government of the people."

"Alexander Alekhine," demanded the judge, "how do you plead?"

Standing there, confronting the hostile faces, hearing for the first time the reason he was there, he stammered, "I ... I am guilty of nothing. I know nothing of any weapons, of any subversive materials. There is some kind of mistake. I have seen neither weapons nor anything else subversive. I deny these accusations. They are completely false! Completely!"

"Proceed with your case, Comrade Prosecutor."

The prosecutor, stroking his mustache as he watched Alex respond, turned back to face the judges. "Our intelligence forces have been following closely the activities of a small group of dissidents, and had reason to believe they were about to begin distribution of subversive literature and weapons. Having been informed of the location where these were believed to be assembled and stored, our forces raided the premises. Their information proved correct. A large trunk full of pistols, ammunition, and inflammatory literature was found. I have given each of you specimens of the writings which were retrieved in the operation. As I am sure you will agree, release of such provocative, false ideas could have serious repercussions."

He waited, giving the tribunal time to examine in more detail the documents before them, then continued, "The only occupant of the room where these were found was the accused, Alexander Alekhine. Upon interrogation, he claimed that two supposedly total strangers had taken pity upon him, and had invited him to spend the night there. These strangers, he stated, were English journalists named Fred Evans and Roger Sloane. No journalists of such names have been admitted to our country. In fact, no English journalists, regardless of name, have been granted entry."

"Why did the defendant say he needed help from strangers?" asked one of the judges.

"That was all part of a fanciful story that he had just, that very day, returned from the war, and had found his home destroyed and his parents dead. With one exception, there is nothing believable in the fairy tale he presented. The one fact in his story is the admission that he is the son of Victor Alekhine, the authoritarian leader of the duma which enacted the oppressive laws against which we had to struggle for so long! Is it believable that by mere coincidence the son of this Victor Alekhine is found occupying a room filled with weapons and vile, dangerous documents designed to sabotage the government of the people? It stretches the imagination beyond the limits of belief!" He sat down.

The atmosphere in the court underwent a sudden change with the revelation of Alex's identification. The judges seemed supercharged as they conferred with animation in low voices for a couple of minutes, after which the one in the center said, "Alexander Alekhine, what else do you have to say in your defense?"

Appalled, Alex struggled to clear his throat, trying to sound calm and convincing. "However strange it may seem, everything I have said is the truth. I had absolutely no knowledge whatsoever of the contents of the trunk. I never saw any of the items alluded to by the Prosecutor. The night I was arrested was my first one in Moscow in more than four years, and truly I had never met those men before. I swear I am not part of any group trying to overthrow the government. I have never discussed any such ideas with anyone, because such ideas have never entered my mind. The war interrupted my career as a professional chess player, and my only interest is in resuming that activity. The fact," his voice suddenly turning infuriated, "the only true one, according to my accuser, is that Victor Alekhine was my father—something which I voluntarily told the Prosecutor. Absolutely nothing else with which I have been charged in this case is true!"

"And that is your defense?" asked one of the judges."

"I am not guilty, as God is my witness. That is all I can say."

"Comrade Prosecutor, have you anything else to add?"

With a scornful glance at Alex, he arose to his feet. "God does not testify in The People's Court. Defendants always claim to be innocent. That this defendant is the son of an enemy of the people may be coincidental, but the defendant's possession of subversive materials is hard evidence. There is no doubt about his guilt. My recommendation is that he be executed."

Executed? In all the gloomy imaginings of his fate during the period endured in his cell, ignorant of the charges against him, the possibility of a death sentence never occurred to him. Incredulous, his eyes locked with those of his denunciator. The naked hatred he saw made him so dizzy he nearly lost his balance.

It took only thirty seconds of conferring by the judges to produce a verdict. "The People's Court concurs with the recommendation that Alexander Alekhine be executed. Within 72 hours after confirmation of this decision, the execution will be by firing squad."

Nine

The prison was a massive, three-story, hollow rectangle built of stone. Except for the solitary arched portal where those entering or leaving had to pass through two sets of heavy, steel-barred gates, no windows or other openings pierced its outer walls. Within the enclosed open area stood a small, two-story structure. On its upper floor, under continuous illumination, were twenty cells, each six by nine feet. Here, those facing execution were housed. Though the cells on this death row were drier and cleaner, an aura of death was pervasive, overwhelming whenever a somber delegation arrived to lead away one of the hapless lot.

Before assignment to a cell, Alex was subjected to having his head shaved, being stripped of his clothes—a notation was made of the fresh, ugly scar on his back—then clothed in pocketless shirt and beltless trousers, with only heavy socks to cover his feet.

The generally abusive, contemptuous attitude of the guards towards the inmates in the cell blocks of the larger structure was absent in the corridor where those to be executed were housed. Here, the guards tended to treat their charges with sympathy, even respect, speaking to them in quiet tones, sometimes offering them lighted cigarettes— inmates weren't permitted matches—listening to those who, on rare occasions, wanted someone to talk to. Most of the time, the condemned spent their hours in brooding contemplation, some in ceaseless prayer.

Disbelieving, confused, devoid of reason, Alex was scarcely aware of what was taking place during the admittance procedure. When finally in his cell, he lay for hours without coherent thought. Terror gradually emerged from the confusion and he trembled uncontrollably. Tears slipped from between his lids until escape arrived in the form of restless sleep...

*He is playing brilliant chess against a huge, grinning
ape, but every time he captures a piece two new ones
appear on the board. In frustration, he kicks over the
board and tries to throttle the animal, but his hands are
not large enough to rip its enormous neck, and he can only
clutch a clump of coarse, greasy hair.*

*"Don't be silly," says the ape, shoving him away so
forcibly that he falls at the feet of Rosa Pereira, who is
playing the Mendelssohn wedding march.*

He awoke, clear-headed and angry—anger directed first at the
anonymous panel of judges, joined by the arrogant prosecutor. It then
shifted focus to Sloane and Evans, and the capricious fate which had
brought him into their clutches. His enraged thoughts continued back-
ward in time to the nightmarish events at the family home, then to the
wounding which had delayed his return, before which were the wasted
years in Lisbon, preceded by the catastrophic aftermath of the Mannheim tournament. Why? He had done nothing to be the recipient of such
punishment. It was at this point that he began beating his head against
the wall, cursing the fate that, above all else, had frustrated him from
his one, lifelong goal—to go down in history as the greatest chess player
who ever lived.

Horrified, he watched at dawn as the door to a cell across from him
was opened and guards dragged away a stumbling, babbling wretch. The
chill within him turned into unmanageable shuddering a few minutes
later, when the burst of a fusillade echoed through the prison yard. Twice
more, during the next hour, the sight and sounds associated with similar departures from nearby cells exhausted his emotional reserves, leaving him unable to move from his cot the entire day. Early in the evening,
new tenants for the vacant cells arrived.

By the following evening, the population of the corridor had decreased;
no replacements arrived for five more prisoners who had made their final
exits.

Tomorrow they come for me, was all that Alex could think.

But when the day dawned, guards paraded past his door repeatedly,
as calls came for others, but not for him. His morning meal arrived as
usual. The guard who brought it said nothing. Puzzled, Alex consumed
for the first time most of the unappealing fare. Afterwards, he paced back

64

and forth, smoking an offered cigarette, and tried to dope out an explanation. Could he have miscounted the days? That night, sleep came more easily...

> *He is trying to play chess, while Rosa stands behind him playing music from The Nutcracker. Each time he touches a piece it turns into a toy soldier which, in turn, comes to life and grows to life-size. Two of them seize him and march him to a wall. He turns and finds himself facing others pointing rifles at him. Bow raised, Rosa is about to lower it as a signal for them to fire. He shouts, "Checkmate!" All of the rifles melt. The music fades away.*

He was awakened by the struggles of the man being pulled from the cell next to his. Positive that this victim had arrived more than twenty-four hours later than he, Alex now knew that he had not lost track of time. He brooded over the situation as the day progressed. Had they missed him by oversight? There was no one who could be interceding on his behalf. He still had no reason for hope. All he knew was that he was alive one more day.

Even the guards seemed puzzled when they glanced at him, as even one more day passed. Then, as he was completing his evening meal, he heard the key turn in the lock. Two guards stood at the open door. "Come, you have a visitor," said one, his expression a blend of curiosity and respect.

They went down the stairs, crossed from the smaller structure to the main building and entered an anteroom, where a man working at a desk looked up.

"This is Alekhine," one of his escorts said.

The man nodded, rose and knocked on a door, opened it and disappeared briefly, then emerged and took Alex by the arm.

"I'll take it from here," he said to the guards. "You can wait over there," pointing to chairs against a wall.

He led Alex into a larger adjoining room. "This is the prisoner you wished to see," he said to the man seated behind a large desk.

"Thank you, Comrade. Wait outside."

He gazed with curiosity at the grimy, haggard young man with the ten-day growth of beard. "Your name?"

For his part, Alex stared in shock at his questioner, a man whose picture he had seen displayed everywhere during his day of wandering in Moscow. Recovering, he answered, "Alekhine, Alexander Alekhine."

"Alekhine, the chess master?"

"I play chess, yes."

Lenin stood up, walked across the room and sat down at a small table on which there was a chessboard with pieces arranged for play. "Let's see if you are whom you claim to be. Sit down."

Mystified, Alex accepted the invitation and sat across from the leader of Russia. What this was all about was beyond him. What he did know, though, was that he did not intend to lose the game, regardless of what might follow. He had never thrown a game, and wasn't about to, even to satisfy the ego of this powerful man with the intense, piercing eyes.

"Shall we draw for White?" Lenin asked. The white pieces were already set up on his side of the board.

"It is immaterial to me. Go ahead and move, if you wish."

Lenin nodded and, after a slight hesitation, advanced one of his center pawns. Ordinarily, Alex knew, he could demolish any amateur chess player without trouble, regardless of strength—and though he did not know it, Lenin was a player of considerable ability—but aware of the effects produced by the agonies of the past week, he knew he would need complete concentration to avoid blundering.

As the game progressed, everything else gradually faded from his mind. After some twenty moves he was able to sacrifice a rook and force checkmate in three moves.

Rubbing his bald head, Lenin stared long at the final position, chagrined, but in admiration of someone who, while under such obvious emotional stress, could still visualize such a brilliant combination. Finally, he lit a cigarette, leaned back in his chair and said, "Tell me about yourself."

This man surprised him. "What do you want to know?"

"Who you are, where you come from, what do you believe, what do you want?"

The deep breath he took lifted his shoulders. He let the air out slowly, then began speaking, "I was born in Moscow, November 19, 1892. My parents were Victor and Agnes Alekhine. My father, as I am sure you know, presided over the Duma in 1914 at the time the war started. After my education by tutors and at private schools I majored in languages at Moscow University, receiving my degree in 1914. The war interrupted my plans to study law."

"What do I believe?" He stopped here, pondering what kind of answer was appropriate. Could it be possible that the right words to this intent listener might save his life? "Until now I have always believed, perhaps naively, what I would become, what I achieved, would depend only on my own efforts, on persevering to reach my goals. I did not change those views, even when I was imprisoned by the Germans, even when circumstances beyond my control interrupted my plans."

His breathing accelerated and his voice seethed as he continued, "But suddenly, I find that these beliefs are just an illusion, because others, for reasons I do not understand, have decided that I am a threat to them, though in truth I have done nothing to harm them and have no interest in doing so. Up till now, the truth is that I have had but one interest, one ambition, one goal, and that is to become the chess master of the world."

Lenin blew a smoke ring toward the ceiling, then said, "But you said you intended to study law. In addition to trying to win the championship, were you planning on a career, following in your father's footsteps?"

"No. That's undoubtedly what my parents had in mind, but I had no interest in it. I agreed to study law, since such knowledge could be useful, but my only target was the chess title. My language studies also tied into that objective, since I would have to be prepared to take care of myself all over the world."

Shifting suddenly into fluent German, Lenin said, "What languages do you speak?"

Changing without effort or hesitation, Alex replied in a flawless accent, "I am told that I speak German, French and English as well as natives of those countries. I also have a good knowledge of Italian, Spanish and Portuguese, but still need to work on them."

In fairly good French, Lenin said, "In what ways?"

Responding in kind, "I need to increase my vocabularies, and to refine my accents."

"You mean, like I do?" Lenin said, in hesitant, guttural English.

For the first time in many days, a hint of a smile appeared on his lips as Alex answered in English, "Our problems would seem to have certain similarities."

His face inscrutable, Lenin reverted to Russian. "What was your relationship with your father?"

Alex's face reddened, his eyes flashed, and his voice turned bitter. "My father? I'll gladly tell you about my father. He was a self-centered, abusive drunk. He was an unfaithful womanizer. He was a compulsive gambler, who lost all of his own large inheritance at Monte Carlo, and tried to do the same with my mother's."

"And how did she deal with this?"

"She was smart enough to keep most of her money out of his grasp, and she always protected me, but the constant strain was so great that she also began to rely too much on alcohol." His mouth was twisted in anger.

"When did you last see them?"

"Not since July 1914. They were trying to talk me out of going to a tournament in Germany, but I went anyway, and ended up a prisoner."

Lenin reflected on that, as he formed another smoke ring. His next question was, "From whom did your mother get her wealth?"

"She was the daughter of Dmitri Prokhoreff."

"Ah, yes. We know about him and his labor practices."

Feeling himself a mouse played with by a cat, Alex watched the enigmatic smile Lenin wore as he carefully ground out his cigarette.

"You say you did not want a political career. Did you have any interest in joining your grandfather's industrial empire?

"No, none. Just chess."

"Even so, you must have some opinions on political and economic theories and practices. What do capitalism or Marxism mean to you?"

Was the cat tiring of the game and ready for the kill? Alex racked his brain, desperate for a suitable answer. "In all honesty, I have never tried to crystallize my ideas on such subjects, because I haven't studied or even read about them. I do not remember hearing my parents discuss such matters as I was growing up, and I probably wouldn't have paid any attention if they did. I suppose I just accepted that the system we had must have been the best one, or else it would have been changed."

Tugging gently at his beard as he listened, Lenin was trying to decide whether this young man who stared at him with such intensity was as artless as he sounded. "Tell me exactly why you were sentenced to death."

Alex steeled himself. This was it, his last chance to appeal. "I am here through a terrible mistake. I returned to Moscow for the first time since 1914, and discovered my parents had been killed and our home destroyed. That same day, two men who said they were from England, saw that I was in a state of shock and tried to help me. They took me to a place where we had food and drink, mostly drink. I don't remember how long we stayed there drinking vodka. Finally, they put me in a room with a bed and said they would return the following day. The next thing I knew, I was pulled out of a drunken sleep by some men—soldiers or police, I assume—who said there was subversive literature in a trunk. If there was, I wouldn't have known. I passed out as soon as we got there. I can only guess that the authorities had suspicions, and I was unlucky enough to be sleeping there when they raided the place. I had never seen or heard of the two men before, and haven't heard from them since. That is the complete story."

"Is there any way you could prove that you had just gotten back to Moscow?"

"I was a patient for several weeks in a hospital in Göteborg until two weeks before. There should be a record of it. A week later I began my trip here."

Lenin lit another cigarette, watched smoke from his lips curling upwards, then turned his gaze back to Alex. "If you hadn't been arrested, what would you have done?"

"I haven't the faintest idea. I wasn't expecting to find myself totally alone and penniless, and I hadn't started to think about my future—or anything else, for that matter. I was just paralyzed."

"I assume you still want to pursue your goal in chess?"

"Yes, absolutely."

"Could you support yourself just playing chess?"

"Once I become champion I'm sure I can. Otherwise, I know of masters in other countries who literally starved to death trying to. I suppose I'd have to find some form of gainful employment."

Lenin again changed the subject. "How did you feel about the war?"

Alex scowled. "I thought the whole thing was stupid. It was an inexcusable waste of lives and resources. For what purpose? Did anyone win anything? It seems to me that Germany will pay a high price for its arrogant greed. France and England lost millions of men. And, as for Russia," here Alex decided to try a gambit, "its obvious lack of preparation exposed the weakness of its leadership. I imagine it will take many years to recover."

"Did you fight in the war?"

"No. While I was held by the Germans I decided that, if and when I was released, I would go to a neutral country and wait it out. That's what I did, not expecting it to go on for four years."

"Where were you?"

"In Portugal."

"How did you support yourself?"

"I translated foreign dispatches for a wire service, and also translated articles for a magazine."

Lenin's eyes briefly widened, then he shifted subjects once more. "How do you feel about Russia?"

"What do you mean? I am a Russian. I feel sad about what has happened to my people."

Lenin now introduced his own counter-gambit. "How do you feel about the change of government?"

Alex decided his fate rested on accepting it. "I don't know what is going on, but I accept that the old system has failed."

For decades, Lenin's success—even his survival—had depended on judging whom to trust. He decided to accept Alex's story. Good use could be made of his talents. "Do you love Russia enough to be willing to help make it better than it ever was?"

Alex had been aware for some time of the pounding of his heart. It now seemed to thunder in his ears. He swallowed hard, tried not to stammer, and blurted, "Of course!"

"Very well, I'm going to accept your story at face value, and give you a chance to prove yourself. You will be given work in the government which makes use of your knowledge of languages. I warn you, though, that if my judgment is wrong, there will be no second reprieve."

He strode to the door and called to the man who had brought Alex to him. "The charges against Alexander Alekhine are to be dropped. See to it that his belongings are restored to him, that he is provided with adequate clothing. Contact the Commissar of the Housing Authority and tell him I said to give Alekhine a room within walking distance of the Kremlin." He turned back to Alex and said, "As soon as you are settled and cleaned up, report to the Commissariat of Foreign Affairs." Without another word he left the room.

Alex, who had risen when Lenin did, sank back into his chair and dropped his head into the midst of the chess pieces.

Ten

The times were turbulent. The Commissariat of Foreign Affairs, still trying to get itself organized, and flooded with ardent, questioning followers, was a madhouse of foreign tongues. In no time, Alex was in demand as interpreter at an endless series of heated discussions. In the midst of continuous excitement, Alex was able to remain calm, detached. His life had been spared. He had food, shelter, employment. When not at work there was chess, where new things were also happening in Russia.

Lenin and Trotsky made chess a political tool, and encouraged its use on a wide scale. It was incorporated as part of military training. It was taught in the schools. Worker organizations were told to form their own chess clubs. The Commissariat of Culture had the assignment to improve the character and intellect of the Russian people through chess, the national game.

"We want you to help," the Deputy Commissar told Alex.

"Gladly. In what ways?"

"Teaching, exhibitions, anything to stimulate interest."

"I have little free time, but could give some evening lectures, and occasional exhibitions."

"Good. Our teaching corps for beginners is adequate, but we need help for advanced students."

"I could play groups of them in simultaneous exhibitions, and analyze the results," said Alex. "Another thing which would stimulate interest would be blindfold games."

"Blindfold! You can play that way?"

"Of course. I can play several such games at once."

"That would be wonderful! I'll check our schedules and get back to you," he said, delighted.

The Commissar doused his deputy's enthusiasm. "Blindfold chess is nothing but a gimmick. It does not help us meet our objectives. We want no part of it. If that's the kind of player this Alekhine is, we can get along without him."

Alex merely shrugged when he received an embarrassed report from the Deputy Commissar. He didn't mind not being called on to help. It gave him more time to work on his own game. It paid off. In 1920, the first All-Russia championship tournament was held. He won it without losing a game. His reputation, limited to the upper classes in 1914, now spread through the nation's masses.

That didn't solve the problem facing him. Russians were not allowed to play abroad. That was where he needed to be. Anxiously, he followed reports of chess elsewhere. The news that serious negotiations for a world championship match between Lasker and Capablanca were under-way was enough to give him intestinal cramps. Liberal consumption of vodka was of little help.

He had to get out of Russia. How? The only way he could escape, it seemed, was as the husband of a foreign national, something highly unlikely. Still, he made it his business to know who would be coming for meetings with the Commissariat of Foreign Affairs.

Opportunity came with a meeting of the Comintern. He was assigned to the meetings of a committee. When a subcommittee was set up for an important task, its chairman asked that he keep notes of its work and help her in preparing the final report. The chairman was Anna Rüegg, an unattached, energetic woman from Prague, who kept an experienced, firm hand on the reins for seven hours of fervent dialectic during the first day. When they adjourned for the day, she asked Alex if he could remain to review the decisions made.

"Of course," he said. "I'm here to serve in any way you wish."

After an hour more, she announced, "That's enough for today. My throat is parched from all this talking. I need a drink."

"If you would like," said Alex, "I can show you a place nearby where you can get anything from tea to exceptionally fine vodka."

She smiled, "The vodka sounds ideal. Lead on."

"Mmm, that's just what I needed," she said, after they were settled at a table, and had sampled the bottle Alex had ordered. "You were right. It is very fine vodka."

"There aren't many places where you can find it," he said, refilling their glasses.

"I'm impressed with your command of languages."

"Well, I've been studying them all my life."

She looked at him inquisitively. "If I may ask, how old are you?"

"Twenty-seven."

Her face turned wistful. "If my son had lived, he would be the same age. He only lived three years."

He shook his head in sympathy. "How tragic. Do you have other children?"

"No, I am alone. No children, no husband." She drained her glass, which he refilled immediately. "It's not easy being alone. If it weren't for the Comintern work, life would be unbearable."

"I can appreciate that. I also have no family. I am thankful to have my work, too."

"But a man your age must have some diversions?"

"My only one is chess."

"No girls? Surely a man with your looks and intelligence should have girls at his heels all the time."

"I'm not quite that fortunate. Even so, most of the young ones I've met seem too frivolous and immature. If I am lucky enough to find an intelligent one, she's usually already committed."

"Or too old, I suppose."

"No. I think women who have seen something of life can be far more interesting companions."

She finished the vodka left in her glass, refilled it herself, and said, "I'm going to have one more than my usual limit, because it is so delicious that I hate to see so much left in the bottle."

"It doesn't have to go to waste. Take the bottle with you."

"Oh, may I? Thank you very much."

"My pleasure."

The next day, they again worked another hour after the committee meeting had adjourned. Then she said, "You have earned a reward. Let's go to my room and finish the bottle. I don't want to drink alone."

There was still a little in the bottle when she took him to bed.

74

Afterwards, as they drank the last of it, she said, "I don't know how you learned it, but you certainly know how to cater to a woman's needs. If my late husband had treated me that way, I would have mourned when he died. As it was, I was just relieved."

He stopped nibbling her neck long enough to say, "I can't imagine that. He gave you no pleasure?"

"None. He was just an animal."

"How stupid! It should be heaven to spend every night with someone as responsive as you."

She clutched him tightly. "You know how to flatter a silly, old woman."

"It's not flattery, and you're not an old woman."

"I'm fifty-one."

"So what? That makes no difference."

"After all, I'll only be away five nights, and then we'll have one more week together."

"Five nights will seem an eternity," he said. "I've gotten spoiled."

"You've gotten spoiled? What about me? The last few nights have been pure ecstasy for me. What I dread is when the job is finished and I have to go home."

"So do I."

Her committee had decided that they would need to go to Petrograd to get additional information before their task could be completed. Another interpreter already there would take over Alex's duties for the group.

Alex spent the time getting ready. He would never have a better chance.

Two nights after the Petrograd trip, she sighed, "I can't stand the thought of going home next week without you, but there's nothing else I can do."

His fingers wandered through her hair. "You're wrong. There is something you can do."

She sat up, surprised. "What are you saying?"

"I'm saying there is a way we can be together."

"How? I want to know."

"Let me come with you."

Her breath caught in her throat. "There's nothing I would want more, but how could you?"

"As your husband. Will you marry me?"

She jumped out of the bed, turned and stared at him, awestruck. "You can't mean that! You're saying you would give up your career for an old woman?"

"How many times must I tell you, you are not an old woman? As for my career, my work here is limited. I can go only so far. I'm sure I could find better opportunities outside Russia."

"You're serious?"

"I've never been more serious."

"Then my answer is yes! How soon can it be done?"

"How about tomorrow?"

She threw herself on top of him, smothered him with kisses, and screamed, "Yes! Yes! Tomorrow! Yes! Tomorrow!"

For most of the interminable journey their trains were infuriatingly slow. Schedules were unreliable. They had to change trains many times, usually with long waits. The ride was bumpy, the air stuffy, and Anna felt sick much of the time. No food was sold on the trains. At scheduled stops Alex usually got off to buy what he could. He tried to find foods and drinks which might help settle her stomach.

He had no travel sickness but, though the law was definite about the rights of the spouse of a foreigner to emigrate, the tight knot in his gut did not disappear until they had crossed into Poland. A sense of triumph enveloped him, but he managed to hide his exuberance from Anna.

The stretch of track leading into Breslau, the last significant stop before the Czechoslovakia border, was very rough. Her relief when the train stopped at the station was so great that she promptly fell asleep, and did not awaken until well after the train was again under way. Some time later, she began to wonder where her husband was. Then she noticed that his suitcase was missing.

Also, she discovered, when she got around to checking, was most of her money.

Eleven

He went to Berlin. It had been the center of European chess activity. He found a room, then headed for its oldest club. Depressed with what he found—broken furniture, ragged rugs, library depleted, lack of maintenance evident, the handful of players all elderly—he turned to leave, only to collide with a rotund figure. "I beg your—Bogul!"

"Alex! I thought you'd be in Russia," said Boguljubov, wrapping him in his arms.

"I was, but have just left. What are you doing here?"

"I've settled in Germany and married a local girl. We live on a farm—she and her brother own it—about an hour from here. But, sit down and tell me what's happened to you since you so mysteriously disappeared from us at Rastatt."

"The details arc too long to describe, but I eventually managed to get out of Germany and back into action with my army unit. I caught some shrapnel in my back, which kept me in the hospital awhile, during which the government collapsed. After I got out, I was put to work by the new authorities as a translator, but soon tired of it and left. I came here to see if this is a good place to make a new start. What do you think?"

"I wouldn't recommend it. The economy has collapsed, and the inflation is unbelievable. We manage, because we grow enough to eat well. That's more than most people can say. In your place, I'd suggest a country that was on the winning side. Opportunities should be there."

His brow wrinkled, Alex asked, "Opportunities in chess?"

"Yes. I've been to a few tournaments in France and Italy, even made one trip to England. There's a fair amount of activity."

"Well, from what you say, and what I see here, I guess I'd better do as you advise. Thanks. I'm glad I ran into you." He smiled. "Now, tell me what happened to you."

"A couple of months after you left, they offered us release if we would work on their farms. The work was hard, but I ended up marrying the farmer's daughter. While I still do a lot of the work, it's usually possible for me to get away to some tournaments."

"In that case, I guess we'll see each other from time to time."

"I hope so," said Boguljubov.

"Before I leave," Alex said, "for old times sake, do you have time for a blindfold game?"

"Of course," was the response, a big smile breaking out on his round face.

Alex sat at a sidewalk table in Paris. He nursed his coffee, as he considered what to do next.

"Alex! Is it really you?"

He looked up, jumped to his feet and hugged her. "Olga! What a surprise!"

"A wonderful surprise! How long have you been here?"

"Since yesterday. And you?"

"Several years. Well before the Revolution. Father was wise enough to see it coming, and we got out."

"Sit down, please, and have some coffee with me. There's so much for us to talk about."

They smiled at each other, waiting for her coffee. Olga Ivanov, a year older than Alex, had lived in the house next to the Alekhines' since both were toddlers. The families were in the same social set and close friends.

"Your parents are well?" he asked.

"Yes. They have an apartment here. I have my own, not too far from them." She sipped her coffee. "And your parents?"

"Dead. Those barbarians murdered them and burned down our home." He watched the horror in her face. Grim, he added, "The same thing happened to your house, as well as to all the others in the neighborhood."

She shuddered. "How awful! I can't tell you how sorry I am." She

78

reached across the table to cover his hand with hers. "You weren't there at the time?"

"No, I was in an Austrian hospital, recovering from a wound."

"Are you planning to stay here?"

"I hope so. I need to get settled, and earn some money."

"Look," she said, "come along with me. The folks will love to see you. I'm on my way there right now. I have dinner with them every Wednesday. They'll have all kinds of questions for you."

"I'd love to see them, too, but I don't want to upset their dinner arrangements."

"Don't be foolish! It won't be a problem."

Her parents were delighted to see Alex, but Mrs. Ivanov cried when he told them what had happened. Ivanov turned somber, but said he had suspected something of the sort could take place. "What about you?" he asked. "Bring us up to date."

"Well, as I told Olga, I spent some time in an Austrian hospital. When I got back to Moscow, and discovered what had happened, all I could think of was retaliation. I affiliated with a small group working to throw the villains out. Passing myself off as a Leninist supporter, I managed to get a government job, where I could get information to relay to the group. It worked for a couple of years, but they finally got suspicious, and I decided I'd better leave while I could."

Ivanov said, "Our White Russian colony is having a dinner meeting Friday evening. Would you come as our guest, and give the group your views on the situation back there?"

"I'll be glad to tell them what I know."

"Fine. There will be others there that know you and will be glad to see you."

"It will be nice to see friendly faces." Additional contacts could be useful.

The size of the crowd surprised him. There were two hundred there, thirsting for information. He had never addressed such a crowd, but was not intimidated. He knew what they would want to hear, and he didn't restrain himself in his remarks.

"Russia is being destroyed," he said. "Lenin and his gang are tearing down all existing institutions. They have appropriated land and other private property, nationalized all banks, abolished the old education system, making their propaganda the centerpiece of all teaching, and are suppressing all forms of dissent. Their aim is to spread their influence to cover all of Europe. I have been present, as an interpreter, at many meetings where such plans are discussed in detail. But all is not yet lost. They control the major cities, but are still meeting a lot of resistance in the rest of the country. It's essential that every individual, as well as the governments of all civilized nations unite to help overthrow these criminals."

When he was finished he was swamped by people seeking information about the fate of missing relatives or friends, but he could tell them little of value. Even so, he received warm thanks from the group, some of whom offered to help him find employment.

Word of what Alex had said quickly got back to the Kremlin. In retaliation, all records of his chess accomplishments were erased.

❖ ❖ ❖

Once settled in Paris, he applied for French citizenship. Olga helped him find an apartment near hers, but the incredibly busy schedule he immediately began dashed any designs on him she might have had. He found work, translating for a news magazine, and enrolled to study law. Before that, he had made contact with the local chess community to learn what professional tournaments were scheduled throughout Europe. Above all, he had to make up for lost time—he was approaching his twenty-ninth birthday—by re-establishing himself as a legitimate contender for the world title. He had lost none of his skill, and recognition came quickly. Within six months he played in three major tournaments, and won first prize in each, without losing a single game.

He had to watch his expenditures. What he earned from the magazine job, even supplemented by tournament prizes and money from exhibitions, would allow few extravagances. To increase his income, despite the physical demands, he gave more exhibitions of simultaneous blindfold play. These brought larger audiences and publicity. He gradually increased the number of such games played at once, though he was not yet ready to challenge the twenty-two game record of Pillsbury's, played in Moscow in 1904, an event he now claimed to have witnessed.

80

"Have you heard?" Janowsky asked Alex. "Lasker has finally agreed to give Capablanca a title match."

"No, I hadn't heard," he said, surprised. "When, and where?"

"Next month, in Havana." Janowsky was the strongest player in France until Alex's arrival. A naturalized French citizen, he had the good fortune to have a friend who subsidized him generously, which allowed him to spend all of his time at chess. "Who do you think will win?"

"Capa, beyond question."

"I agree. If he wins, will you challenge him?"

"I don't care who is champion. I'm going to beat him."

"Maybe you can. I don't think anyone else around would have a chance. Your problem, though, is to get him to play you before you die of old age."

"Don't I know it?" was Alex's grim response.

"By golly, Alex, it's great to see you! Eight years is a long time."

"Too long, Frank. Eight years before I could thank you for helping me to get away from the Germans."

"No problem for me. You still have some change coming from the money you gave me."

"Forget it. It was a good investment."

"How did your mother get you out? I want to hear the whole story."

"She went to her father, who was the one who managed it. The story will have to wait till some other time. First, what's this I hear about you having your own club?"

Marshall struck a match with his thumbnail, lit the cigar he'd been chewing on, and said, "Yeah, we wanted a place where fellows could get together to play and get some instruction—sorta like Simpson's Divan here in London. We started at Keene's Chop House. It was so popular," he said, pausing to puff on his stogie, "that we soon needed larger quarters. We've had to move a couple of times, and now operate out of a house. I say we, because it couldn't be done without my wife, Caroline. She keeps everything running. All I do is have fun."

"It sounds great. I'd like to see it."

"Come on over. You're more than welcome."

They were in London for a major tournament, one which attracted more than usual interest because it would be the first time the new world champion would be participating in such competition since giving Emanuel Lasker a bad beating in their match. Behind 10–4, Lasker didn't bother to finish it, resigning it to escape muggy Havana.

"Look who's coming," said Marshall, "the Champ himself."

Alex turned, a welcoming smile on his face.

"Alekhine! Good to see you," Capablanca said. Alex thought he detected a new note of condescension in the greeting.

"Hello, Raúl, it's been awhile. Congratulations on winning the championship."

"Thanks. I hear you have been playing well."

"Well enough, I think, to give you a workout. How about a match?"

White teeth gleamed, as the Cuban grinned. "I'd be delighted, but you'll have to get in line. Others have applied ahead of you, but I'll play whoever can first meet the requirements. It makes no difference to me."

"What are your requirements?"

"I'll announce them to everyone at the end of the tournament. Now, if you'll excuse me," he said, consulting the gold watch attached to a heavy gold chain across his chest, "I'm scheduled for a press interview."

"Don't look so glum, Alex," Marshall said, watching Capablanca walk off. "Royalty must meet its responsibilities, no matter how burdensome."

"That supercilious air really gripes me. I thought we were pretty good friends, but after eight years, he doesn't have a minute to give me the time of day. Some day I'll take the conceit out of him. Mark my words."

"It won't be easy. He hasn't lost a single game in the last five years."

"Well, maybe we'll end that record this week."

"I'll be rooting for you, but remembering what he did to me in our match, I won't put any money on you."

The field of sixteen grandmasters there in London was the strongest group assembled since before the war. Interest was high. Should anyone succeed in outperforming Capablanca he was sure to be considered a leading challenger for the crown.

Alex had reason to feel confident. Of fifty tournament games since

82

leaving Russia, he had won thirty-five, losing only one. Most of those in the know figured that he, if anyone, had the best chance to win the tournament.

Their judgment was justifiable. Alex didn't lose a game, finishing with eight wins and seven draws. Unfortunately, even with the advantage of playing White, he could only manage a draw in his game with Capablanca. That wasn't good enough. The champion was also undefeated and had drawn only six games, thus finishing a half-point ahead of him.

Accepting the first prize at the post-tournament banquet, Capablanca announced that the details of his requirements for future championship matches would be released the next day at a press conference. Would-be challengers were invited to attend.

"I should get first crack," Alex said to Marshall, "but I'll bet I don't."

"I agree, though Rubinstein also has a legitimate case. After all, only the war kept him from the match Lasker had promised him."

"Yes, but now he's past his prime. I can handle him."

Cigar in mouth, Marshall said, "Capa's not afraid of anyone, but he's no dope, either. I think he'll stall for time by putting Rubinstein ahead of you."

"Why?"

"Why? Because Rubinstein could have more trouble finding backers willing to put up his stake. Remember, also, you've still never won even a single game from him, as José Raúl will surely be careful to remind everyone. Anyway, you might as well stop stewing about it until you hear the rules tomorrow. Relax, and enjoy the musical we've been invited to see. They tell me the girls in it are an eyeful."

That was true. Capablanca, as always, watched them with appreciation, picking out the one he hoped to entertain later in the evening. As for Alex, he didn't bother to look at them, sitting through the entire performance with his eyes glued to his pocket set, as he replayed his game with the Cuban, trying, without success, to figure out how he might have beaten him.

A dozen grandmasters, as well as a number of representatives of the press, were assembled at eleven o'clock the following morning to hear Capablanca's pronouncements. He strode in on the dot, an impressive, handsome figure in his perfectly fitted dark suit.

"Gentlemen," he said, his smile brilliant, "it is a pleasure to see so many of you. I promised to make my conditions for a title match known today, and here they are. First of all, anyone wishing to issue a challenge shall submit it in writing, together with a good-faith, non-refundable deposit of five hundred dollars. If the match takes place, that money will be used to help defray expenses of the sponsors. If the match does not occur, the money shall belong to me. The challenger shall be responsible for obtaining acceptable sponsors of the match, who shall guarantee a purse of at least fifteen thousand U.S. dollars. Two-thirds of the purse shall be awarded to the winner of the match, with the loser to receive one-third. The sponsors shall be responsible for all expenses involved in putting on the match, including transportation for the contestants and for their personal expenses during the competition, as well as for the site where it is held. Each contestant may have a second, if he wishes. The sponsors need not be responsible for the expenses of the second. The challenger shall have six months after issuing his challenge to secure the required sponsorship for the match. If he is unable to meet this time limit, he shall lose his chance, and the next challenger will be given his opportunity."

"He's certainly protecting himself," muttered Alex. "I don't know of anyone who would put up that kind of money for a match. No one in Europe has that much free money now."

"You'll have to cross the Atlantic to find it, and I advise you to do so," said Marshall. "If you..."—he stopped as Capablanca continued reading his rules.

"Draw games in the match shall not count. To win the title the challenger must win six games before I do, but with one proviso. If the score is tied at five wins apiece, the challenger must win two more games. If I tie the score at six wins each, the title shall remain mine."

Several masters present shouted, "That's unfair!" and an angry murmur went through the room.

"I'm sorry if you find that objectionable," the Cuban said, his smile tight, "but those are my conditions. I believe my overall record justifies that, on the basis of a single match, I be defeated by a margin sufficient to prove that the result was not just a fluke."

Alex was fuming. "Whatever that bastard's rules, I'll beat him when the time comes. And I mean that," he added, aware of Marshall's skeptical expression. "It will be different, I guarantee!"

"The site for the match, as well as the rules of play and other details, shall be negotiated by the contestants together with the sponsors." Capablanca paused, then added, "I am leaving copies of these specifications on the table. If you plan to issue a challenge within the next year, send a copy to me by the end of next month, with your signature to show that you will accept these requirements. Thank you, gentlemen." He turned and started to leave.

The reporter from *The Times* jumped to his feet. "Mr. Capablanca, aren't you going to answer any questions?"

"I see no need to. There is nothing to add."

"Will you at least explain why your match requirements differ from those used in your match with Dr. Lasker?"

"The explanation is simple. Every titleholder before me set his own rules for championship matches. I have set my own." With that, he walked out, ignoring others who were shouting questions.

"The emperor has spoken," said Marshall.

"That prig!" said Alex, incensed. "Wait till I get him. I'll knock that smugness out of him!"

Marshall lit a cigar as they walked to the door, after picking up copies of the match requirements, then said, "You haven't asked for my advice, Alex, but I'm going to give you some, whether you want it or not. First, though I think your chess now is the finest I've ever seen, it doesn't work against Capa. He knows how to stifle your attacking style. Second, though you've been cleaning up in Europe, if you want to get a title shot you've got to come to America and make a big impression there. That's the only way anyone with money will back you. And you should get over there as soon as possible."

"Thanks for the advice, friend. You're right, as usual. I'll come as soon as I can, but can't until I finish my law studies in June. As for my style of play, I realize it will have to be changed. All I can say is that whatever has to be done, I'm prepared to do it."

"Let me know when you'll be ready to come, and I'll try to pave the way for you."

"Thanks, Frank. It's nice to have someone I can depend on."

Twelve

Dear Frank,

Thanks for your letter of the 14th. Yes, I did receive my degree. Henceforth, you must address me as "Doctor" and treat me with due deference! Tomorrow I sail for Montreal, where I shall begin a series of exhibitions in several Canadian cities extending over a period of three weeks. If everything goes according to schedule, I should reach New York around the 20th of August, at which time I hope to learn that your efforts to find financial support for a match have borne fruit. I'm truly grateful for your help.

Before leaving Canada I'll send you my exact date of arrival so that you can have a brass band on hand to greet me!

Kindest wishes,
Alex

Her bobbed red hair tossing in the breeze, Mae stared moodily at the water. Her companion's grumbling didn't help. "I know, I know. I'm sure it would have been better on the *Mauritania*, but it wasn't my fault that it was completely booked."

"This is a total bore," said the blonde. "I've never been on a crossing with so few interesting men." She opened her gold case, took out a cigarette and fitted it into a long, ivory holder.

Mae watched the flame on the gold lighter blow out time after time. "You'll never get it lit in this wind, Lucy. We might as well go back to the lounge."

"Just a minute," Lucy replied, seeing the tall, mystery man with the widow's peak approaching.

Alex stopped. "Allow me," he said, taking the lighter and shielding the flame successfully with his hands, as he lit her cigarette."

"Oh, thank you. I never could have done it," she said, giving him her biggest smile.

"Not at all," he said, with a formal inclination of his head to each of them, and resumed his rapid pacing along the deck. Disgusted, Lucy watched him disappear.

"Anyway, you got your cigarette lit," Mae said.

"I wonder what's wrong with him?"

"I guess we're just not his type."

One of the few unattached men on board, they had been aware of him ever since the first night, when they saw him dining alone at a table near theirs, totally absorbed in the book he was studying. His obvious deep concentration—he even appeared unaware of what he was eating—was enough to discourage any thought of a contrived interruption. It was the same at every meal. Except for three brisk walks each day, Alex was giving no time to anything but chess. When not exploring chess theory, the puzzle of how to win backing for a match against Capablanca monopolized his thoughts. There was no break in his routine until the final day, when his turn and privilege to dine at the captain's table was scheduled. He would have been glad to do without the honor, but accepted the invitation on the off-chance that a useful contact might result.

In his formal wear—necessary at major tournament banquets—he was the last to arrive, and found his place card at the foot of the table. He was amused to note that the captain, twice his age, was flanked by two, pretty young things—he recognized them as the ones he had seen on deck when he stopped to help one light her cigarette—while neither of the women next to him would ever see sixty again. Both, however, were beautifully gowned and lavishly adorned with jewelry of obvious value. Using her lorgnette to help read his place card, the woman on his left, an American named Mrs. Bowman, asked, "Dr. Alekhine? You are a physician?"

"No, Madame, I hold the title of Doctor of Laws."

"Oh, where did you study?"

"At the Sorbonne."

Lucy and Mae strained to hear what he was saying, while feigning interest in the captain's account of his experiences.

The woman on Alex's right, whose place card said Nadyezhda Vasilief, broke in. "But you are not French, are you? Isn't Alekhine a Russian name?"

"Yes" he said, with a smile, "but I recently became a French citizen. Am I correct in assuming that you are also from Russia?"

"Yes, but I'm afraid I'll never be able to go back. My late husband, General Gregor Vasilief, was killed fighting the accursed Bolsheviks."

"I'm sorry to hear that. So many brave men have died fighting to restore sanity to that misguided nation."

He turned and faced Mrs. Bowman. "Many of the finest people have chosen to leave Russia. Their one hope is that the present regime will soon collapse, and that reason will prevail, allowing them to return."

"My goodness, I should hope so! My husband," she nodded toward a man seated across the table from her, "says that the men in power are a bunch of criminals who will end up fighting each other, and that their whole system will fall apart."

Alex nodded. "Yes, they are criminals, but I'm afraid they've become so strongly entrenched that they may be able to survive internal strife for quite awhile."

The Russian woman said, "The wealth of the nation is being destroyed or stolen."

"As I well know," said Alex, the bitterness in his voice apparent. "Our home was burned, my parents were murdered, and their land seized. Now, I am left with nothing, and must go looking for financial support."

Mr. Bowman, a fat and florid man, with a voice that carried well past their table, entered the conversation. "Support for what, young man?"

Everyone at the table, even the captain and his companions, listened.

"I am looking for someone to sponsor a match for the world's chess championship."

"Chess? You must be kidding! What fool would waste hard-earned money so a dozen people could stand around watching a couple of guys sit at a table motionless for hours?"

Alex's face grew even redder than Bowman's. "There are people who waste money—as you put it, sir—on paintings because they appreciate the art of the brush. I believe I can find some who also appreciate the art of the mind, and are willing to gamble on their judgment."

Bowman snorted. "You won't find them in the good, old U.S. of A.! If you are talking about something like a championship prize fight, that would be another matter. That's where American men are willing to gamble on their judgment."

"Thank you for your opinion, but I do not intend to give up," was his angry response.

Nadyezhda Vasilief said, "In the old Russia, chess ability was greatly admired. It was evidence of culture and intelligence."

Her support calmed him. "Thank you, Madame. Your own culture and intelligence are also evident. I'm sorry that we didn't meet earlier on this voyage. I should have enjoyed more of your company."

"Thank you, but I am too old to believe such flattery."

"It's not flattery, and age has nothing to do with it. It is clear that you are an interesting woman."

She laughed. "I'm beginning to think that you are persuasive enough to find a sponsor for a chess match, regardless of what that gentleman says. I shall watch the papers, and if you succeed I'll be in the audience."

"With that incentive, I know I will," he answered, and picking up her hand—getting a close-up view of her heavy, diamond and ruby bracelet in the process—he kissed it, as everyone else at the table looked on in surprise.

Back in their cabin, Mae said, "Imagine it, a date talking about chess. What a thrill!"

Unfastening her dress, Lucy said, "I'll bet I could get his mind off chess."

Mae laughed. "Maybe, but he seemed to prefer that old woman."

Thirteen

"May I help you?"

The question came from a slender, dark-haired woman of around forty seated at a small table just inside the entrance to the Marshall Chess Club on West 12th Street.

Removing his hat, dripping from the cold rain he had just escaped, Alex bowed slightly. "Would Mr. Frank Marshall be here? I am Alexander Alekhine."

"Oh, Dr. Alekhine," she said, a smile of pleasure appearing as she extended a welcoming hand, "I've been looking forward to meeting you. I'm Caroline Marshall. Frank has told me so much about you."

"I'm happy to meet you, but I shall have something to say to Frank. If he had even hinted that he had such a charming wife, I would have arranged to get here much sooner."

"Thank you," she said, laughing, "but even if it were true, it wouldn't have happened. Frank has never been known to talk about anything but chess."

"A failing to which I am also susceptible."

"Frank should be back soon. He just stepped out to buy some cigars. Let me have your hat and coat. Would you like some hot coffee? I can have some ready in just a few minutes."

"Yes, that would be very welcome. It's quite a chilly morning, colder than it was in Montreal yesterday."

"While I'm getting it, perhaps you'd like to look around the club while it's still empty. We don't open until eleven."

It had evidently been a private home. Now, three downstairs rooms had been furnished with comfortable mahogany arm chairs and small

90

tables, each with an inlaid chessboard. Mounted on the walls were dozens of photographs of individuals prominent in the chess world, as well as sketches or paintings of centuries of chess lore. In the entry hall, beside the table, was a large bulletin board displaying the results of various tournaments or matches, and announcements of coming chess events at the club or elsewhere.

On the board was also a clipping of a recent interview with Frank which had appeared in a Sunday edition of a New York paper. Alex was reading it when Caroline reappeared with coffee for both of them.

"That's quite an interesting article," he said.

She laughed. "Frank didn't want me to put it up, because it says he looks like a Shakespearean actor."

Alex examined the photograph accompanying the text and said, "You know, that's right. I'd never thought about it, but he'd make a perfect Hamlet."

They were seated at one of the chess tables, savoring the coffee, when they heard the door slam.

"That's Frank. He always slams the door," she said.

Alex rose and walked to the hall where, puffing on a cigar, Marshall was hanging up his wet coat.

"Something is rotten in the State of Denmark! It must be Hamlet. I'd recognize that smell anywhere."

"Critics everywhere. Now I know that clipping has to come down. How are you, Alex?" Marshall answered, his grin wide, as he shook hands with enthusiasm.

"I'm fine, thanks. These are nice quarters you have here."

"We've only been here about a year, but the way the club is growing it looks like we'll have to find a bigger place before long. Have you met Caroline yet?"

"Yes, we've just been enjoying coffee in the next room. How were you ever so lucky to find a wife like her?" he asked, as they entered the room where she was sitting.

"Oh, she was the brilliancy prize I won at a tournament," was the answer, as he leaned over to kiss her cheek.

"That's not true," she said, laughing. "I was the trophy for the biggest blunder."

"I've made my share of blunders, but winning you wasn't one of them."

She stood up. "After that, the least I can do is get you some coffee."

"Tell me about your Canadian adventures," Marshall said, when the men were seated.

"It was pretty good, I thought. I was surprised to find so much interest in chess everywhere I went. There were at least fifty boards in each simultaneous, and in Montreal and Toronto I faced more than a hundred. Some of them were quite good players."

"How did you do, overall?"

"In the six exhibitions, I played 423 games altogether. I lost seven and had draws in thirty-one. That doesn't include the blindfold games."

"You did some of those, too?"

"Yes, on separate nights I played blindfold in four cities, ten games at once in each case. I lost five and drew eleven out of the forty games."

"Not bad. Not bad at all. That should have made an impression."

"Yes, it did generate a good deal of press coverage. Did any of it make the New York papers?"

"I saw a couple of brief items, but our press doesn't give much space to chess, unless it's a local event."

Caroline, who had rejoined them, said, "I'm sure we can arrange some interviews for you with most of the major papers here."

"Thanks, that would be very useful. Frank, what's the word on possible backing for a match with Capa?"

"Not good. The people here with enough money to meet his demands just aren't interested in chess. It looks like only someone putting up his own money can corner Capa, and I don't know of any chess master that well off. While you can make dough with an exhibition tour, it isn't going to be anywhere near enough. Maybe the only answer is to rob a bank—that, or marry a rich woman."

Caroline, seeing Alex wince, protested, "Oh, Frank! I can't believe it's that bad. If Dr. Alekhine gets better known here through exhibitions, and wins a big tournament, I'll bet someone would show up to back him in a match."

Alex frowned. "Is there anything in the works for a tournament?"

"Nothing big, but if I give some people a little shove, it might be possible that something might be put together by early summer, maybe even late spring. I'll look into it. Meanwhile, Caroline is right. You should be able to do your cause some good, and earn a little in the process, if you go on a nationwide tour. I'd think you'll find as much interest as you did in Canada."

"Well, unless you can find me that rich wife—I don't think I want to try robbing a bank—I guess I'd better go ahead with an exhibition tour. I can't afford to wait around six months for a tournament, and I don't want to go back to Europe without getting at Capa one way or another. Is he around here now?"

After relighting his cigar, Marshall said, "No, with winter coming on, he's basking in the Cuban sun, and enjoying the way his country-men fuss over him. I think they'd elect him president of Cuba, if he'd let 'em. He won't, 'cause he's too lazy to ever do any real work."

"Meanwhile, he keeps out of reach. How about Rubinstein? Any signs he may be finding a backer?"

"Nope. He's no salesman. With his personality, I doubt he'd ever find supporters, whatever his playing ability."

Alex swallowed the last of the coffee in his cup, then asked, "How would you suggest I begin organizing my campaign here?"

"I think Caroline's idea of some press interviews would be an excellent way to begin. You can use those to announce your plans to do an exhibition tour. Stories in the New York papers are seen in most major cities, and that should start generating some invitations. I'll make some calls, as well, and that should get the ball rolling."

Fourteen

Boris Geller, Associate Professor of Slavic Languages at Johns Hopkins University, looked across the kitchen table at his mother. The tea they had been drinking was strong, the way he knew she liked it.

"Is there anything you'd especially like to do? Museums? Shows? Shopping?"

"Not particularly. I can get as much of those things in New York as I want. I just came to see you. Besides, as miserable as the weather is, I'm happy to stay indoors. You don't have to entertain me, and I don't want to interrupt any plans you have. I'll be quite satisfied here by myself, reading or listening to the radio, if you want to go anywhere on your own."

They hadn't seen a great deal of each other during the past twenty years, but now that she had an apartment in New York, she was looking forward to more frequent, even if brief, contacts with him. As he turned to reach for the teapot, the light from overhead reflecting on his bald spot reminded her of how much, at forty-two, he resembled his father. He had the same round face, ruddy cheeks, blue eyes, and thick straight eyebrows. The only thing missing was his father's bristling, brown mustache.

"Except for morning lectures tomorrow and Friday, I'm pretty much free of commitments until you leave on Sunday. There's just one date I'd like to keep. If you are agreeable to being alone Friday evening, I have plans to go to the Faculty Club, where I have the opportunity to be one of forty to play against a renowned young chess player."

"Oh? What's his name?"

"He's a Russian named Alekhine. Many people think he could be the next world champion."

"He will be. I'm sure of it," she said. The expression of surprise which developed on his face amused her.

"What—what makes you say that?"

"I know, because he told me he would."

"Told you? You know Alekhine?"

"I sat next to him at the captain's table on the ship, the night before we reached Montreal. He told me all about his plans, and I must say he's a very convincing and impressive young man."

"I'll be damned! What a coincidence. I'll have to remind him of it when we meet. I was one of the committee that arranged for his exhibition here."

"Would it be possible for me to come along to watch? I'd like to see how you do against him."

"Sure, that's no problem. But you could get pretty tired of it after a little while. The exhibition could go on for four or five hours."

"That wouldn't bother me. I know enough about the game to be able to understand what's happening, and if I did get bored, I imagine there is someplace at the club where I could sit and read."

"Yes, there is a library next to the dining room, where we'll be playing."

"Good. I've never seen an exhibition like this. I'll be interested to see how it's done."

The forty opponents were seated on the outer rim of tables arranged in a horseshoe. Each was identified by a card on which his name had been printed.

Reaching Boris's board, Alex nodded, "Mr. Geller," and was just about to advance a center pawn when his eye caught the smiling woman standing behind his adversary.

"Madame Vasilief! What a delightful surprise!" he said, his hand suspended in midair. "I didn't expect to see you here."

"Dr. Alekhine, you do have a remarkable memory for names. I'm here to see how my son, Boris, performs against you," she said, holding out her hand, which he grasped with enthusiasm.

"I never forget an exceptional woman," he said to Boris. "If heredity means anything, I see I'll have to play with extra care against you." Then, before releasing her hand, he told her, "Thank you for coming. I hope you won't be disappointed."

"You must have made quite an impression on him," Boris said to his mother, after Alex had moved several boards along.

"He made quite an impression on me."

Once the games were under way, Alex never raised his eyes from board level, except when he shook hands with a defeated opponent. All of his adversaries except four were eliminated within three hours. Boris was one of the survivors. Reaching him on his thirty-eighth round of moves, Alex offered Boris a draw, which was gladly accepted. Then to the mother, who was now seated beside her son, he said, "I was right. Your son plays a fine game. It was a double pleasure, playing him and seeing you, as well. I hope it will happen again."

"I'm just visiting here. I live in New York."

"I'll be there soon, myself. A big tournament will be held there in a couple of weeks."

"If you have time, I'd be glad to have you call me."

"I'll be delighted to. Is your number listed?"

"Not yet, but I can write it down for you."

"That won't be necessary. Just tell it to me. I won't forget it."

Fifteen

"Nineteen cities in eleven weeks? Not bad. You've seen more of the United States than ninety percent of the population see in a lifetime."

"Yes, I suppose so," Alex said, waiting for his coffee to cool down.

"What did you think of it?"

"Of what, Frank?"

"Of the scenery, the cities, the food, the people. What were your impressions of our great country?"

Alex thought about this for awhile. "I guess I was struck most by the friendliness and energy of the people, and by the enthusiasm of the chess players I met, though they represent only such a very tiny part of the public. My impression is that few native-born Americans have any interest in the game. It's not as much a part of the culture as it is in Europe."

"Sad to say, that's true. Most people here look at us woodpushers as curiosities, wasting our time, when we could be doing something worthwhile. But, what the hell, I feel sorry for them. They don't know what they're missing. Money is all they think about."

Alex sputtered, choking on the coffee he was sampling. "Yes, but even we poor chess players need money, too, at least enough for room and board. Speaking of which I can't say much for the food here."

"Knowing you, I'm surprised that you even noticed what you were eating, since your nose is seldom out of a chess book. I'll bet you didn't even see much of the scenery as you traveled."

"You know me well. That is true."

"How about the tour? Did you run into much competition?"

"A few times, though I think I met more strong players in Canada.

I've been told that almost all the really good U.S. players are here in New York."

"That's right. It's the only area where players get the chance to develop against tough competition."

"What's the latest on the tournament?" Alex asked, after a sip of coffee.

"It's all set. Eleven players, double round-robin. The big news is that Rubinstein couldn't make it over here, so Lasker—Emanuel, that is, Ed is also playing—was persuaded to take his place."

"That's a surprise. After his sorry showing against Capa in Havana, I thought he had decided to retire. At his age he should."

"Yeah, but he's a proud old guy, and I guess he wants to show the world he isn't washed up."

"Who else is playing?"

"You and I, both Laskers, Capa, Réti, Boguljubov, Yates, Maróczy, Janowsky and Tartakower. Not bad, eh? Except for Rubinstein, that's as strong a group as could be assembled anywhere."

"Yes, the cream of the crop."

"If you do win this tournament, maybe some interest could be generated for backing you in a title match. If so, I don't think Capa could put anyone else ahead of you, regardless of his so-called 'rules'."

"Well, that's what I'm here for, and that's what I'm going to do."

As Marshall began unwrapping a cigar he smiled and said, "I hope you can, but don't expect me to throw our games. I may just decide to win that first-prize money myself. I could use it."

Alex laughed. "More power to you. If I beat Capa you can have the money."

After his friend had the cigar lit and drawing to his satisfaction, Alex asked, "Where is the money for the tournament coming from?"

"The credit for getting this one on the road belongs to Harry Latz. He's the general manager of the Alamac Hotel, where the tournament will be held. He's not only furnishing the hall where we'll play, he's giving all the out-of-town contestants free accommodations for the five weeks the affair will take. To top it off, he's contributing twenty-five hundred bucks to the prize fund."

"He sounds like a true chess lover."

"He is. I can add that he is the one person I've found who has said he would help finance a match against Capa. I'm pretty sure he could be persuaded to put up at least the same amount."

"I'm glad to hear that. I'd like to meet him."

"I'll see that you do, in the next few days."

By the end of the second round, having beaten Frederick Yates, Britain's strongest player, and Géza Maróczy, the Hungarian champion, Alex stood alone in first place in the New York tournament of 1924, the most important one the United States had hosted in decades. This happy situation was too good to last. Aging ex-champion, Emanuel Lasker, capitalized on a series of inferior moves by Alex, brought on by over-confidence, and won their game easily.

"Serves me right," Alex confessed to Marshall at dinner, that night. "I must be more careful from now on."

He was. The end of the first round-robin found him ahead of everyone except the surprising ex-champion. What most frustrated Alex, though, was that he again failed to get better than a draw against the reigning champion.

Marshall urged him to look on the bright side. "So, you didn't beat Capa this time. Even so, you're ahead of him and get another whack at him. Beat him and Emanuel in the next round and you'll be home free."

It wasn't to be; he only got draws with each of them. To make matters worse, Alex lost his game with Réti, the Czechoslovakian master. Meanwhile, Capablanca came to life. When it was over, the tenacious Dr. Lasker had won the $1500 first prize, ahead of Capablanca, with Alex a dejected third.

After the closing ceremonies, Marshall, happy with his $500 prize for finishing fourth, again tried to raise Alex's spirits. "You're still ahead of everyone else. Whenever Capa does agree to a match, you have to be considered first in line."

"He's not looking for a match with anyone, especially me. Did you hear what he told the press after the tournament? He said he was disappointed in the showing of the 'younger generation.' That crack was aimed just at me. No one else fits the description. What hypocrisy!"

Sixteen

The following morning, Alex received a telephone call.

"Dr. Alekhine? Boris Geller speaking."

"My Baltimore opponent?"

"Yes, though I'm here in New York at the moment. I had hoped to see more of the tournament, but was only able to get here for the final round. Your game with Tartakower was very interesting to watch. I thought you had the edge."

"Yes, but not enough to win."

"Even so, your overall performance was outstanding."

"Thank you, but it was a disappointment to me. I had hoped for better than twelve draws in twenty games."

"My reason for calling, Dr. Alekhine, is to find out whether you would be free this evening to dine with my mother and me?"

"This evening? Thank you. It will be a pleasure. At what time?"

"We'll pick you up at the Alamac at 7:30."

"Fine. I look forward to seeing both of you, and shall be waiting at the door."

"You are very punctual," Alex said, as Boris emerged from a taxi.

"Thanks to the efficiency of the doorman at Mother's apartment," he replied, as they shook hands.

"I'm happy you could join us," his mother said, holding out her hand to Alex.

"I'm delighted for the opportunity. It's a welcome change to be with people whose company I enjoy."

"Weren't any of the others in the tournament friends of yours?"

"Yes, most of them are—some even close friends—but there is often an undercurrent of rivalry, which tends to inhibit complete relaxation."

"Will you be leaving New York soon?" she asked, after they were seated at their table at Luchow's restaurant.

"No, not for awhile, Madame Vasilief, I have been engaged to prepare an analysis of all of the tournament games for inclusion in the commemorative book to be published, they hope, before the end of the year."

"In that case, I expect you to keep your promise to call me, and please, don't be so formal. My name is Nadyezhda."

He beamed. "You can be sure that I will, Nadyezhda, and very soon, so that I may repay the hospitality I owe you both. And, my friends call me Alex."

"Unfortunately, I won't be here for that, Alex," said Boris. "I need to get back to Baltimore tomorrow."

"Nevertheless, you must come back for an occasional weekend, when we can get together. Meanwhile, I won't wait to call your mother."

"And we shall have much to talk about," she said. "So much, I think, that we'll have to converse in Russian and French, as well as English."

"She's not fooling," her son said. "Russians love to talk, and Mother is a true Russian."

"So am I, and I always will be, even though I now hold French citizenship."

"I, too," she said. "I would love to return to Russia, but I won't, not as long as those Bolshevik animals are in control."

"Nor will I," said Alex.

Four days later, after two hours of nonstop conversation at the Russian Tea Room, Alex and Nadyezhda stood just inside the open door to her apartment.

"Thank you for a wonderful afternoon. I can't remember when I've enjoyed myself that much."

"The pleasure was mine," he replied.

"You're a dear boy to give so much time to an old lady," she said, rising on tiptoes to kiss his cheek.

"Everything you just said is wrong," he said, embracing her. "I am

101

not a boy, you are a vibrant woman, and I'm not giving, I'm taking." With that, he kissed her firmly on the mouth, and as her lips opened in surprise, she felt his tongue caressing hers.

Their feet collided as, without releasing each other, both of them tried to kick the door closed at the same time.

He put aside the paper he was working on to answer the telephone. "Hello."

"Dr. Geller?"

"Yes," he said, recognizing the voice of the university switchboard operator.

"You have a long distance call from Atlantic City."

"Atlantic City?" That was puzzling. Who could be calling him from Atlantic City? "All right, put them on."

"Boris?"

"Mother? What are you doing in Atlantic City?"

"Enjoying myself, as one should. We're here on our honeymoon."

"Honeymoon? What on earth are you talking about? Who's we?"

"Alex and I. We were married this morning."

"Alex! You can't be serious!"

"Of course I'm serious."

"But … but, you're too old to be—good lord! I'm ten years older than he is. And you tell me he's my stepfather? That's—it's obscene!"

"Oh, Boris, you are such an old fogy, just like your father! Our ages don't matter. We love each other, and that's all that matters. If you had ever married, you'd have known."

"Maybe I would have, if I didn't also have to help you keep up your kind of lifestyle. I hope Alex can take over that chore, but I doubt it. Chess professionals rarely earn enough just to keep themselves alive, let alone support a wife."

Her voice grew icy. "I'm sure we'll manage. We certainly don't intend to be a burden to you."

Before he could say anything, she had hung up. Angry at himself for what he had just said, he wanted to apologize, but didn't know where in Atlantic City they were staying. Overwhelmed by the impact of her call, he sat there without hanging up the receiver until the switchboard operator interrupted his reverie to ask if he wished to place a call.

Alex, lying on the rumpled sheet, stopped examining a small mole below his navel to ask, "Burden? What was that all about?"

"Oh, the news just caught him by surprise. He'll get over it after he gets used to the idea."

"But what was that business about managing? Have you been dependent on him for support?"

"He has been helping with some of my expenses," she confessed, as she sat on the side of the bed and began running her hand along the inside of his thigh.

"Such as?" he asked, placing his hand over hers.

"He takes care of my clothing bills, and pays the rent on the apartment." She tried to continue moving her hand, but his pressure was too strong. "We don't need him, do we?" her voice suddenly anxious.

"No, I won't let you starve, my love," he said, trying to hide his sudden consternation. "But until I win the championship, my income will be unpredictable and sometimes less than I'd like, so we'll need to be prudent about how we spend. I've never asked you anything about money, because I intend to support us both. That's my responsibility."

"I'm sure you will, sweetheart," she said, pressing her cheek against the hand holding hers.

"I assume," he said, the fingers of his other hand combing through her silver-streaked, luxuriant hair, "that your previous husbands made some provisions for your future?"

She straightened up, and pursed her lips. "David Geller, Boris's father—did I ever mention that he was an admiral—had enough foresight to put something aside for Boris and me. He lived several years after retiring, and received a generous pension. After he died, I continued to receive half of it, until the Bolsheviks took over. Then, it just stopped coming without any word of explanation. As for General Vasilief, whom I married in 1912, he believed in spending every ruble he had. He was generous, and gave me a lot of jewelry, but that was all. After he was killed in action in 1915, I discovered he had left nothing but debts, and had made no arrangements for survivor's benefits with the government. David evidently didn't believe I could manage the bulk of his estate properly, and he left it to Boris, with the understanding that he would see to it that I didn't starve."

"From your end of the conversation on the telephone, I gathered that he now considers himself relieved of that responsibility."

"He did sound that way," she admitted, "but I'm sure he'll help if we ask."

"I'm not in the habit of asking anyone for help, and I don't intend to start now. I'll take care of our needs." It was the first time she had ever heard him sound angry.

"I know you will, darling, and I promise not to be extravagant. I don't need anything except you," she said, as she leaned over and kissed him.

His face grim, he held her tightly.

Seventeen

"Married?" Frank Marshall exclaimed. "I'll be damned! Who's the lucky girl?"

"Her name is Nadyezhda Vasilief. She is a widow."

"Where'd you meet her, if it's any of my business?"

"I met her on board ship coming over here. Then, to my surprise, she was in the audience watching my exhibition in Baltimore. It turned out that one of my opponents was her son, a professor at Johns Hopkins University."

"You aren't planning to live in Baltimore, are you?"

"No, for the time being we're living in Nadyezhda's apartment here in Manhattan. After I finish doing the analyses for the tournament book, we intend to make our home in Paris."

"Tell me about her," Frank said, flicking ash from his cigar into a large ashtray.

"She's a fellow Russian, well-educated, intelligent and with a charming personality. Her first husband was an admiral, the second a general. As you can guess, she's an older woman. Actually—it probably seems strange to you—I'm younger than her son. That doesn't matter to me. I find mature women more interesting."

Marshall managed to hide his surprise fairly well, though his eyes involuntarily spread. "I look forward to meeting her."

"You and Caroline both shall, I promise, and soon. I know you'll both like her. Now, though, I'd like your thoughts on something else. Even though my tour in this country went well, my results in the tournament weren't good enough. Before I leave, I want to do something which could galvanize public interest and support. What if I were to try to break the record for simultaneous blindfold games, competing against, say, twenty-six of New York's strongest players?"

The idea brought an enthusiastic response from Marshall. "Hot damn! That would really take some doing. You'd be willing to tackle something that tough?"

"Yes, it's an idea I have been considering for some time, because of the prestige it would bring and, now that I'm a married man, I could use extra money."

"It's a lollapalooza of an idea." He released a large cloud of smoke. "I'll call Harry Latz right now. I think he'd be interested in putting it on."

Latz was intrigued. "I think that's a fantastic idea. I'll be glad to provide the hall for you, and I'm sure I can enlist others to publicize it and contribute to the financing. What kind of a fee do you have mind?"

"I wouldn't want to try this for less than five hundred dollars," Alex said.

Latz's brows knit briefly, then he nodded. "Okay, I'll personally guarantee it."

Caroline was astonished. "Alex married? And you mean it when you say she's old enough to be his mother?"

"Alex told me she has a son older than he is."

"It seems unbelievable! I can't imagine him doing something like that."

"I can. I think I may have given him the idea when I said he could get quick money by marrying a rich woman, or robbing a bank. He ruled out the robbery."

"I don't know. I can't visualize Alex marrying just for money."

"I can, knowing how obsessed he is to beat Capa."

"I hope we'll get to meet her soon. I want to see what kind of person she is."

"So do I. Alex says she'll charm us."

There was concern on her face and in her voice. "Do you really think you should, darling? Couldn't the strain on your mind and nerves harm you?"

Alex smiled. "Don't worry, love, I'll survive."

106

"Is the money that important?"

"It will come in handy, but no, that's not the main reason. When I was nine years old, I watched Pillsbury set a record, playing twenty-two blindfold games at once. I've always dreamed of breaking that record and doing it against even stronger opposition."

"All the same, I'm going to be watching. If I see that it requires too much effort, I'll stop the whole thing."

"You can be in the audience, if you wish, but no one—not even you, sweetheart—should ever even think of interfering with anything I do in chess. I wouldn't be responsible for the consequences. But, all that's going to happen is that you'll be bored stiff after five or six hours and wishing that you'd stayed home."

"Never! I'm your wife and I'll be there to the end, no matter how long it takes."

The sounds of early afternoon traffic on 71st Street came through the open window Alex faced. He sat in a comfortable, brown, leather armchair. Two pitchers, one of ice water, the other of hot coffee, rested within reach on a table beside him. Also on the table were two packs of cigarettes, a silver table-lighter, and a large ashtray.

Behind him, at two long, parallel tables, twenty-six chosen representatives from the leading Manhattan and Brooklyn chess clubs awaited the start of play. The six from the prestigious Manhattan Chess Club and an equal number from the Marshall Chess Club included the names of many of the best-known amateur players in the country. Harry Latz, Frank Marshall and Edward Lasker stood between the long tables. A capacity audience sat on chairs mounted on platforms installed for the occasion.

Latz went over and conferred briefly with Alex, then turned and addressed the spectators. "Ladies and gentlemen, welcome to the Hotel Alamac where, on this rare—historic, we hope—occasion, we are to have the privilege of watching the eminent Dr. Alexander Alekhine try to set a new world record by playing twenty-six simultaneous games of chess without seeing any of the boards. This test is particularly noteworthy because he will be competing against the strongest group of players ever assembled for a blindfold undertaking. Assisting in this exhibition as monitors will be two gentlemen who rank among the world's finest exponents of the game, Frank Marshall and Edward Lasker. In this contest, as Dr. Alekhine announces his moves, Mr. Lasker will repeat them for confirmation and will make the move on the appropriate board of the games on the table on my left. Mr. Marshall will do the same at the table on my right. When Dr. Alekhine has completed his opening move for each of the games, the monitor will return to the first board to observe, then call out the opponent's move, which must be made immediately upon his arrival. Dr. Alekhine will respond, with the same procedure being followed in turn at each of the games in the rounds which follow. Except for ten-minute rest periods at approximately two-hour intervals, play will continue until about seven o'clock. If, as seems likely, games are still in progress, there will be a one-hour recess for dinner. Following dinner the competition will be carried on until all games are completed. Needless to say, since he will need to keep track of 832 pieces being moved around on 1664 squares, the audience is expected to do nothing at any time to interrupt Dr. Alekhine's concentration. Now, Doctor, you may begin when ready."

Alex, playing the white pieces in all of the games, called out his moves in a firm voice, using three different opening moves for variety. During the first few rounds, his responses to his opponent's moves were usually made without hesitation, the positions being well-known. Gradually each game became distinctive, and his moves required more careful consideration.

Twenty-three games were still in progress when Alex took his first break. Two of his opponents had found themselves in hopeless situations within a dozen moves and had given up. Alex had resigned the other game even sooner, because he had overlooked a move threatening his queen. He had anticipated that he could make such a blunder, and forced himself to forget it and concentrate on the remaining contests.

He stood up, stretched, leaned out the window for a minute to look at the activity on the street below, poured a cup of coffee, then lit his fifth cigarette of the session. After resting five minutes, without ever having turned around, Alex told Latz he was ready to resume play as soon as the others were.

At seven o'clock, before beginning the dinner recess, Alex said that he wished to verify the positions on the remaining boards. Scarcely hesitating, with Marshall and Lasker confirming him, he quickly called off the position of every piece still standing in the eleven games remaining in progress. When he completed this, without an error, the audience responded with a standing ovation.

Nadyezhda, who had watched every minute of the performance, joined him in the private dining room provided by Harry Latz, where they were his dinner guests. Marshall and Lasker were the only others present.

"That was marvelous!" she exclaimed, hugging him. "I can't imagine how you do it."

"Were you there all the time?"

"Every bit of it."

He laughed. "I don't know how you did that, either."

The three men congratulated him, each shaking his hand with enthusiasm.

"That was a great performance," Edward Lasker declared, "and locating the remaining pieces at the end was an inspired touch. You made it seem so easy."

"It actually was easier than I anticipated," said Alex. "I guess I've been blessed with a born knack for it. I can recall the moves of almost every important game I've ever played."

Latz looked at him in amazement. "You can't mean that!"

"Oh, it's true. I can vouch for it," Marshall said.

When they were seated at the table, set with the hotel's finest silver, china and glassware, Latz asked Alex, "What would you like to eat? I didn't know what you would want at this point."

"What I'd really like is a glass of red wine, which I suppose isn't possible, because of the insane prohibition law in this country. As for food, just something light, such as an omelet, and maybe some fruit."

Latz gave the food orders to a waiter, and disappeared briefly. Alex's eyes lit up when he returned bearing a bottle of exceptional French burgundy. "Ah! Civilization isn't entirely gone here after all!" he exclaimed.

Well past midnight, after more than nine hours of playing time, Alex conceded a draw in the final remaining game. Overall he had a record of sixteen wins, five losses, and draws in the other five games. Though losing even a single game under any circumstances was always painful to him, he did admit to Marshall a few days later, and after reading the unanimously laudatory press reports, that it was a creditable performance.

He hoped it would help stimulate future support for him in his campaign for a title match.

It had no effect on Capablanca, relaxing in Havana, however. At the end of the following week, the Alekhines sailed for France.

Eighteen

"Look at this." Coming in with the morning mail, Caroline Marshall handed an envelope to her husband.

"Ah, Capa answered promptly," he said.

She pointed to the stamp. "Look."

"I'll be damned! They've put his picture on their stamps! Can you imagine anything like that happening here in the U.S.?"

"He must really be a hero in Cuba."

"Yeah. I've heard that he's mobbed everywhere he goes down there. Let's see what he has to tell us."

He began reading the letter. "He's turned down our invitation to give an exhibition. Says new responsibilities are demanding too much of his time."

"Responsibilities? Capa? That's hard to believe. Enjoying himself is the only responsibility I think he has ever felt."

"Well," Marshall said, after reading the rest of the letter, "it seems that he now has a job."

"Job? He's never worked in his whole life."

"He has just been made, quote, Minister Plenipotentiary and Envoy at Large of the Republic of Cuba, unquote, and says he will be traveling extensively on goodwill missions."

"Mercy me! Now he really will begin enjoying life!"

She was right. Capablanca set out on a tour of the capital cities of Europe, where the Cuban embassies saw to his comfort, arranged the social functions he requested and negotiated with local chess organizations for exhibitions in accordance with his instructions.

He was an ideal representative of his country. Handsome and socially at ease, he was warmly received and entertained everywhere he went, with hostesses competing to have him as their guest. Occasionally, he deigned to take part in tournaments. Though he feared no player, he never seemed to enter tournaments in which his principal challengers might be playing.

"How did you do in Monte Carlo?" Alex asked Janowsky, who had just returned from a tournament.

"About as I expected. Won third prize, then lost it all at the tables."

Alex laughed. "I know just what you mean. I've learned my lesson at such places."

"By the way, I bring you regards from the eminent Capablanca. He said he was sorry you weren't there."

"I'll bet. Somehow, he never seems to be playing wherever I am. His diplomatic duties always seem to interfere."

"I'll say one thing. He must be doing well at his job. He is popular everywhere he goes, except with the other chess players. He doesn't seem to have much time for them."

❖ ❖ ❖

The champion did make it a point, though, to always be readily accessible to the press. Whenever he met with them the question of a defense of his title would be first on the agenda. His response, his smile sad, was invariably that no one in sight seemed able to inspire enough support to meet the financial conditions for a match. Meanwhile, until there was money on the line, he would just have to be patient.

Signs that the patience of the public was waning began showing up. Articles appeared suggesting that, even though he clearly outclassed everyone else, he was unwilling to put his crown at risk. Indignant, the leading Havana paper ran an editorial recommending that he squelch such nonsense by playing a challenger, any challenger. His hand was forced when an Argentinean newspaper carried the story that several businessmen in Buenos Aires were offering to provide the necessary funds for a match to be held in their city.

At an interview in Copenhagen, Capablanca announced that he would accept a challenge from whomever performed the best in a tournament to be held in New York in 1927.

Only slush remained from the snow which had given Paris a white Christmas, but there were still some slick spots on the sidewalks, and Alex walked cautiously to protect the integrity of the load of wine and brandy in his arms. At his front door he set down the precious cargo with care before getting out his keys.

Hearing him enter, Nadyezhda called from the kitchen that the mail was on the dining room table. A letter bearing Frank Marshall's return address caught his eye. He put the bottles on the table, and without removing his coat or hat, tore open the envelope.

"Is there something wrong?" asked Nadyezhda, seeing the expression on his face, as she entered the room.

"No, but I'll have to start packing. I'm going to New York."

"New York! When? Why?"

"A tournament I must enter. This is the time I absolutely must win. Capa is through hiding. Frank says he has definitely committed himself to a match with the winner."

"When does it start?"

"In early March, but I want to get there ahead of time to prepare."

"How about me? Don't you want me with you?"

"Of course, but the trip could be quite rough in January, and you could be sick all the way."

"I want to go anyway. You shouldn't have to be concerned with anything but chess, and I can keep you free from other problems. Besides, it will give me a chance to see Boris."

A letter of apology had been waiting for them when they had returned to Paris after the 1924 blindfold exhibition in New York. Subsequently, Boris began sending her a check each month equivalent to the amount he had been providing before her marriage. Life was far more comfortable for the Alekhines as a result.

"All right, if you wish, but I won't be very good company. I'll have to concentrate completely on every opponent. I can't let anyone finish ahead of me."

"Your disposition won't bother me, as long as I can be with you.

113

And I know you'll win this tournament. You've won every one in Europe during the past three years, haven't you?"

"Winning those means nothing to Capa. This is the only one that counts."

The competition was as tough as it had been in 1924. It included such masters as Nimzovich, Spielmann, Vidmar, Maróczy and Marshall, but Alex outscored them all—and won the brilliancy prize for a game against Marshall—all, that is, except Capablanca, who finished first. To his chagrin, Alex again failed to win a game from his Cuban foe.

At the conclusion of the post-tournament banquet, a smiling Capablanca rose and said, "As you know, a group of gentlemen have offered to sponsor a title match in Buenos Aires, and accordingly, I have expressed my willingness to make such a match for the world championship available to whoever performed the best in this tournament. Thus, Dr. Alekhine, who had the highest score—aside from my own—is entitled to be the challenger, if he wishes. Do you, Alex?"

"Absolutely!" said Alex, standing up. "It will be a privilege, and I accept with pleasure."

Everyone applauded, as photographs were taken of the two shaking hands.

"I'm proud of you," Nadyezhda said, hugging him as soon as they were back in their room, "and so happy for you! I know how much reaching the top means to you."

He held her tightly. "But I haven't, not yet. I've been climbing all my life, but the hardest part of the climb still lies ahead."

"It won't stop you. I'd bet my life on you."

He gave her a searching look. "I believe you really mean that. Now, I don't dare lose."

"So, you're finally getting your chance," Marshall said, the following day, as he and Alex sat drinking coffee fortified with bootleg Canadian whiskey. "Now all you have to do is win six games from a guy you've never beaten even once in—how many games have you played him?"

"Thirteen," was the scowling response.

"He's remarkable. In the last ten years Capa has lost only one game—the one to Réti in the '24 tournament. He clobbered me in our match years ago. He seems to play without any effort, just like a machine. His chess isn't exciting, often it isn't even very interesting, but it gets the job done. He never makes a mistake, so he never loses."

"You're wrong. He does make mistakes. I've seen games of his that he should have lost, but his opponents—myself included—failed to punish him."

"And in your match you're going to?"

"I damn well am! You can be certain of it."

"Sorry, pal, but I'm never certain of anything."

Alex glared at him. "No one's chess is flawless, and I can prove it. Will you let me copy the games you played in your match with him?"

"Sure. Glad to. That was the worst whipping I ever took, and it wasn't for any lack of trying. If there were any weaknesses in his game, I couldn't find them, and you've got to admit I'm no slouch."

"Granted, but I'm going to use a scalpel and dissect every game Capa ever played, until I find a way to beat him."

Marshall smiled, blew a smoke ring and watched it grow as it moved across the room. "Good luck. I'll help you as much as I can, but to be completely honest, I still can't see betting against him."

Alex stared at his coffee awhile, then said, "Would you consider serving as my second in the match?"

Marshall shook his head slowly. "I was afraid you would ask that. I wish I could, but it wouldn't be fair to Caroline for me to be away so long. The club demands a lot of work and I can't leave it all to her. Besides, I couldn't afford it. As you'll remember, Capa's conditions stated that the sponsors would not be responsible for the expenses of a second. I doubt that you could pick up that added expense, either."

"No, I must admit. I'll just have to make other arrangements about a second. In any event, I do want to thank you for everything you have already done for me."

"No thanks necessary. Whatever I did was because I wanted to."

Back in their hotel room, Alex told Nadyezhda they would be making a change in their return trip itinerary. "We're going to go home by way of Lisbon."

"Hello?"

"Lupi? This is Alex."

"Alex! Where are you?"

"Here in Lisbon. How are you?"

"I'm fine. What brings you to Lisbon?"

"I came to see you. Would you have any free time soon?"

"For you I am always free. Would you like to come by the office, say about four o'clock?"

"Great. Will it be okay if I also bring my wife?"

"Your wife? I didn't know you were married. Bring her, of course. I'd love to meet her."

"Thanks. I'm sure you two will like each other. We'll be there at four. Are you still at the same location?"

"Yes. No change."

Well-mannered and sophisticated as he was, Lupi was barely able to hide his surprise on his first glimpse of the elderly woman accompanying his friend. "Alex," he said, throwing his arms around him, "it's been a long time. How long? Has it really been ten years?"

"That's right, ten years."" He stepped back. "This is Nadyezhda, the lady who has kept me sane for the last three years."

"I'm delighted," he said, taking her proffered hand. "Anyone who can keep Alex sane must be a remarkable person."

"Thank you. From what Alex has told me, you have also had a beneficial effect on his sanity. I'm grateful that you persuaded him not to become cannon fodder in that terrible war."

"It was selfishness. I didn't want to risk seeing his artistry lost."

"I'm selfish, too, and thankful. If it hadn't been for you, I may never have met him."

"Now, sit down, both of you, and tell me what I can get you. Coffee, tea, or one of our select wines? Nadyezhda, if I may call you that?"

"Of course, I want you to. After everything Alex has told me of your wines, I'd love to sample one."

"Great. We won't even bother to ask Alex."

He quickly produced a bottle of white wine, and after each had a glass, he raised his and said, "To this happy reunion."

"Tell me," said Alex, after savoring the wine's taste, "what happened to all that thick, curly hair?"

"I wish I knew," Lupi said, putting his hand up to cover part of the bare scalp above his forehead. "I suppose it went wherever yours did."

"At least I still have some in the middle."

"Yes, I imagine that your chess opponents are intimidated by that spear pointing at them. Is that the secret weapon you intend to use against Capablanca? If so, I hope it works. I'd love to see you beat him."

"Enough to help me do it?"

"If I can be of any help, just ask."

Alex emptied his glass, set it down, and said, "That's why we're here. I need a lot of help, and I feel you are the best person to give it."

Lupi refilled Alex's glass, topped the others, and sat back. "How?"

Alex drew a deep breath, glanced at his wife, and turned back to Lupi. "I don't know whether you remember it, but a dozen years ago you said Capa's games looked as though they were turned out by a lathe, while mine resembled something produced with a mallet and chisel."

"I remember that well. It's still true."

"I've tried thirteen times to win a game from him, but never succeeded. It's clear that my methods don't work, so I have to change my approach if I'm to win our match. What I have to do is learn how to use a lathe, and use it better than he does.

Lupi gave him a very intent look. "You're probably right, but do you think you can make such an adjustment in your ways of thinking?"

"I must. That's why I'm here. It won't be easy, but with your help I want to build a better lathe and learn how to use it."

The sound of Nadyezhda's breathing was all that broke the silence for a long moment. Finally, Lupi said, "What do you propose?"

"How much time can you spare?"

"The demands on my time are usually not great, and I have considerable flexibility."

"Here's what I'd like to do, if you agree. We will return to Paris and sublet our apartment, then return here immediately, and stay until we leave for Buenos Aires in late August. I'll spend all of that time analyzing every game Capa has ever played, learning how to copy his style, while trying to uncover its weaknesses. I want to use you as a sounding board, as much of the time as you can give. What do you think of the idea?"

Lupi turned to Nadyezhda. "What do you think of it?"

117

"I have complete confidence in Alex," she answered, "and I am totally in favor of what he suggests. He knows you. He says he will succeed with your help. That's enough for me. I hope you will agree with his proposal."

Lupi smiled. "After that vote of confidence, what else can I do but say 'yes'. As for time, I imagine I can give as much as you want. I assume you will prefer to work out basic ideas by yourself, before testing them on me?"

"That's right," Alex agreed.

"In that case, I think I can be available for a few hours several afternoons a week, and most evenings."

"Wonderful!" said Alex, jumping up to grab Lupi's hand in both of his. "I knew I could depend on you."

Nadyezhda beamed.

Lupi refilled the three glasses. "We must drink to the success of your plan."

Standing, they clinked glasses and drank.

"We'll start for Paris tomorrow and be back as soon as possible, within ten days, I hope. We'd like to find a small apartment near here, preferably not in the area where I lived before, since we'd like to avoid steep hills."

He didn't add that he also wanted to avoid a neighborhood where he might encounter Maria or Rosa Pereira.

"I'll make inquiries," Lupi said.

"I have to hand it to you," Lupi commented, early in August, "you have Capa's style of play down to perfection. I wouldn't have thought it possible. It will be interesting to see how he reacts to it."

"I hope it confuses him. If I can create some self-doubts in his mind, I think I can beat him."

"I would enjoy seeing that."

"I wish you'd be there as my second. It's a shame that no expense money is provided for seconds."

"How long do you think the match will last?"

"It's anyone's guess, but I have a feeling one of us will be knocked out by the fifteenth game. If so, it should be over within a month."

Lupi leaned back, his expression serious, and appeared to be scrutinizing the ceiling for cracks. His survey completed, he straightened up and said, "At the last meeting of our board of directors, our company decided we should explore the potential for expanding our South American export business. After considering various options, they decided that beginning in September I should spend a month or so looking into the possibilities in Argentina. Since I'll be there at that time, it wouldn't be too burdensome for me to also act as your second, if you'd want me to."

"May I ask who recommended Argentina?"

"I don't exactly recall," Lupi said, straight-faced.

"I'm sure you don't, you old fraud!" and they both exploded in laughter, as Alex stretched across the desk to grab Lupi's hand. "Now, nothing can stop me!"

Nineteen

September in Buenos Aires. The bud Nadyezhda placed in the lapel buttonhole of Alex's jacket came from the beautiful arrangement of spring flowers the match sponsors had sent her.

"Now you will look just as smart as Capablanca."

"How smart I look doesn't matter. It's how smart I'll be."

"No one is smarter than you. You will win, I know."

"Well, at last, the time has come to find out. Let's go. Lupi is waiting at the theater."

The match director, Argentina's leading player, nodded to the men standing in the wings at opposite sides of the Teatro Real. The audience broke into cheers and applause as the contestants, escorted by match sponsors and seconds, approached the brightly illuminated table located front and center on the stage, and shook hands with each other and then with the director.

"Hello, Alex," the Cuban said, smiling graciously. "I hope we have a good match."

"I'll try to accommodate you," Alex responded, pale-faced and features frozen.

"Gentlemen," the director said, "you both know the rules for the match, and the spectators have them explained in their programs, so I will wish you both well, and," with pawns of opposite colors hidden in his fists brought from behind his back, "ask Señor Capablanca to choose."

The defending champion pointed to the left fist and was rewarded with White and the first move.

"Ready?" he asked, and receiving a nod from Alex, advanced the pawn in front of his king two squares, and pushed the button to start Alex's clock.

Having already decided that he would respond to that particular move with the French Defense, Alex instantly moved his own king pawn one square, and pushed the button which stopped his clock and started Capa's. The match was under way. Under the rules, each player was allowed two-and-a-half hours on his clock to make at least forty moves. Games not completed in five hours were to be adjourned until the following day, with the final move written and held sealed by the match director until play resumed.

Almost five hours had passed when, no trace of a smile remaining, Capablanca studied Alex's forty-third move, shook his head slowly, then held out his hand. "You have finally won one, Alex. Congratulations."

"Thank you," Alex said, and rose to accept the applause in the still-packed theater.

Lupi was exultant. "Wonderful, Alex! You really operated that lathe with skill."

"Thanks. It's a relief to have finally won a game from him, after all these years. We can't be sure about my lathe technique until he opens with a queen pawn. I was surprised at his opening today."

"I think he was trying to catch you off-guard, but it backfired."

Nadyezhda, still clinging to his arm after having hugged and kissed him with fervor, said, "It won't matter how he opens. Alex will win."

"What about dinner? Where would you like to eat? This calls for a celebration."

"No. If you don't mind, I think I'll just go up to the room and unwind. Nadyezhda and I can order something through room service. We can get together for breakfast. I'll call you in the morning."

Throughout the months spent in Lisbon, his twice-daily brisk walks had been the only interruptions to his study of Capablanca's games. However, to further prepare himself physically for the match, he did reduce drastically his alcohol consumption, limiting himself to a single glass of wine with his dinner. Resisting the temptation to celebrate his win, he confined himself to that one drink while they ate in their room that evening. In bed later, even after sex with Nadyezhda, he was unable to stifle the continuous review in his mind of the moves of that first game. Sleep eluded him until in desperation he got up and gulped down a large brandy. After two hours of restless sleep, he got out of bed and paced the floor in the dark.

"What is it?" his wife asked, awakened when he crashed into a chair.

"Sorry I disturbed you. I've got a blasted toothache."

She turned on a bedside lamp, got up and rummaged through one of her cases.

"Here, put some of this paregoric on your gum."

The opiate reduced the pain enough to allow him a few more hours of rest, but he was in a foul mood when they got up.

"What damned luck!" he fumed. "How am I going to play today in this condition?"

"Aren't you allowed several postponements without penalty?"

"Yes, but I'd rather save them for study, in case Capa comes up with something new."

"Well, at least call Lupi and discuss it with him."

Lupi didn't think he should risk playing under the handicap of a toothache, and persuaded Alex to let him request a one-day postponement so that he could see a dentist.

Two minutes later, Lupi returned Alex's call. Fortune had smiled. Before he could call the tournament director, the gentleman had called him to notify Alex that Capablanca had asked for a postponement of one day. "How about that?" Lupi crowed. "Losing a game was too much for him! He wants time to regroup."

Despite the pain, Alex was elated. "Fantastic! What a break! It gives me a chance to get a dentist to do something about my tooth."

"Did this just begin last night, or has it happened before?"

"I have had some twinges off and on for a couple of months, but thought it could wait till after the match."

"That was a mistake. I wish you had mentioned it to me. I'd have had my dentist look at it."

"I just felt I couldn't spare the time. Anyway, I'll get to a dentist this morning."

"Would you like me to go along with you?"

"No, thanks, that won't be necessary. Nadyezhda will be with me."

122

"Okay, give me a call when you get back."

"I will. Incidentally, don't mention it to anyone."

"Don't worry. I won't."

Nadyezhda was furious with him. "Why didn't you tell me your tooth was hurting?"

"I didn't see any point in having you worry."

"No point? I'm your wife. You shouldn't keep such things from me."

Relieved by the unexpected free day, they went to a dentist recommended by the hotel management. The dentist quickly dampened Alex's spirits. "You really have neglected your teeth. When did you last see a dentist?"

"I can't remember," Alex confessed. "I promise I'll take care of the problem as soon as the match is finished. Just give me something to stop the pain until then."

"When will that be?"

"In a couple of weeks or so, I imagine."

"Weeks? Impossible!"

"The only thing which will keep the pain from becoming unbearable is to have them out."

"Out? Them? You mean more than one?"

"Six of them should come out without delay."

"Six!"

"Two of them must come out today, beyond question. The others within a week or ten days, at the very latest."

Alex turned his face full of woe to Nadyezhda, who had stood in the room during the examination. "What do I do?"

She looked to the dentist. "If you extract the two today, can you keep the pain under control for a week?"

"I believe so."

"Don't you have a three-day recess next week?" she asked Alex.

Glum, he nodded.

"You'd better follow his advice. Otherwise, you couldn't possibly play tomorrow. I'd think a three-day rest after the others are removed may be enough for you to continue. I remember that I was able to get along a few days after I had several of mine pulled." She turned to the dentist. "Would you agree with that?"

"Yes, I would think so."

Alex grunted. "Okay, go ahead. Yank them out. You wait in the next room," he instructed his wife.

Though for different reasons, it was two uneasy and cautious men who faced each other across the table the next day. Capablanca, customarily content to counterpunch and simplify the position until discovering the slightest weakness to exploit, decided the first game had been a fluke. It would be foolish to depart from what had made him the most successful player of all time. Alex, keeping his dental problems secret, prudently chose an opening almost guaranteed to yield a draw. His opponent, also satisfied for the moment with such an outcome, created no waves, and the game ended without a winner after only three hours of sparring.

"Is the pain very bad?" asked Nadyezhda.

"Not like it was. It's just a dull ache, as long as I use the medication."

"It surely must affect your concentration?"

"I managed today, and I'll do it again tomorrow. I have to."

Mindful of the first game, the champion opened the third one more conservatively by advancing the queen pawn. The strategy turned out to be sound and, the next day, after the seventh hour of play, he evened the score by patiently capitalizing on minuscule edges in position.

"Well played," Alex admitted, turning down his king and extending his hand. He left the stage quickly and rushed to his room without bothering to wait for his wife and Lupi, who had watched the entire contest.

"You'd better not come up just now," she told Lupi. "Let me calm him down."

He nodded. "I'll wait for a call."

Alex entered their room, slammed the door, picked up the first object at hand—Nadyezhda's ivory-bound Bible—and hurled it across the room, where it struck the dresser mirror and bounced into her assorted cosmetics, knocking a perfume bottle to the floor and scattering face powder over much of the dresser top.

Coming into the room, she noted the mess, as well as the almost empty glass of brandy he clutched. Walking over to him and putting her hands on his shoulders, Nadyezhda said, "Try not to take it too hard, love. You'll still win the match. That was an unbelievable performance, considering the pain you had to endure."

"Pain or not, I shouldn't have let him outplay me that way. I can't let it happen again!"

The three-day recess followed the fifth game. It, like the fourth, was an uninspiring draw.

Sitting down for game six, Capablanca was startled by his opponent's gaunt appearance. The pressure must really be getting to Alex, he concluded, as they exchanged the ritual handshake before the opening move. The game ended in yet another draw. Alex had yet to win a game playing the white pieces.

A reporter commented in his column the next morning on the apparent exhaustion of Alekhine, and of how his mouth worked constantly as he pondered his moves. He might have written a vastly different story had he known that Alex's tongue was ceaselessly searching the six unaccustomed spaces now in his mouth. The acute pain was gone, but a dull throbbing reminder of the extractions still persisted when the seventh game began. Nadyezhda, with Lupi's backing, had begged him to use one of his days off, but he refused. When he was beaten in only thirty-one moves, he knew it had been a poor decision, and requested a one-day postponement of the next game.

Buoyed by the enthusiasm of the partisan Latin-American audience and with confidence restored by his second win, Capablanca returned fully relaxed and content to play his regular game. He was certain that his strategic abilities would eventually prevail. No longer distracted by pain, though, Alex demonstrated a surprising patience of his own, and matched the Cuban move for move.

After the first game disaster, Capablanca started games only with the queen pawn. To everyone's surprise, Alex did the same. The spectators found themselves subjected to a display more of prudence than originality. Games Eight, Nine and Ten were unexciting draws. Puzzled by his lack of success, Capablanca stumbled. Before he could recover, he had lost both the eleventh and twelfth games. Alex was back in the lead.

"I must hand it to you, Alex. When you said you were going to beat Capa at his own game, I had my doubts. You are proving it."

"If I am, we'll credit it to your help in teaching me how to operate a lathe. The strategy will work, if I can keep my patience."

As a result, more draws, sometimes tedious, followed. The press grew increasingly critical, attendance began to fall off, and the promoters became more and more unhappy about mounting expenses. Capablanca, now aware that he had failed to prepare adequately, used those complaints as an excuse to suggest that it might be better for all concerned to abandon the match and start over again the following year. Alex, confidence growing daily, refused to even discuss such an idea.

After eight consecutive drawn games, Alex won the twenty-first game decisively, again with the black pieces. The score was now four games to two. Desperate, the defending champion called for another postponement—the last to which he was entitled—and worked feverishly to find a new strategy. Following seven more draws, Capa narrowed the margin to a single game, prevailing in a titanic struggle lasting almost ten hours.

"I'm glad there's another three-day recess," Nadyezhda said to her weary spouse. "You can use a rest."

He swallowed some wine. "Yes, but I think Capa needs it more than I do. He played magnificently today, but I feel he is close to the breaking point. The recess may postpone when he'll cave, but even so, I'm sure I'm going to win in the end."

He and Lupi spent most of the three days analyzing the games he had won, reviewing where he had found the cracks in his opponent's defenses.

His estimate of Capa's reserve capacity proved correct. The champion managed two more draws, then lost the thirty-second game. The end was in sight.

The morning following the adjournment of the thirty-fourth game, in which Alex had sealed his forty-first move, the match director received a message from the Cuban, who did not bother to put in an appearance to congratulate the new world champion, Alexander Alekhine.

Twenty

"How is she?"

His face haggard, Alex shook his head. "I'm sorry you didn't get here in time. She died last night."

Boris Geller's lips compressed, as they eyed each other. Alex opened the door wider. "Come in. Let me have your hat and coat."

"That damned ship had all kinds of problems, and took two days longer than it should. I left the day after your cable arrived."

"It wouldn't have made any difference to Nadyezhda," said Alex, ushering him into the parlor, and pouring a large brandy for each of them. "She was in a coma for the last four days."

Boris sipped his brandy, then asked, "What happened? Did she suffer much?"

"Last month she insisted on accompanying me, as always, to a tournament. It was in Athens, and lasted two weeks. A couple of days before it was over she had a stomach upset, which she thought was from some shellfish. She stayed in the cabin most of the time during the trip back to Marseilles, and seemed better once we were on the Paris train. She felt all right the next couple of days, then suddenly just collapsed."

He drained his glass, set it down, and continued, "The doctor prescribed some medicines and bed rest, but admitted her condition puzzled him. Nadyezhda was aware, though, that something was seriously wrong, and asked me to notify you. Meanwhile, a consulting doctor was brought in, but he didn't have anything new to offer. They have decided death was caused by liver failure, but I think that is just to avoid an autopsy, which I wouldn't want, either."

"I agree. It couldn't bring her back." Boris had more of the brandy, then grimaced. "My relationship with her hasn't been very good these past few years. I guess we were both somewhat at fault, but I'm sorry I didn't make more of an effort to improve it."

"I think she felt the same. She told me that if we returned to the United States again, she was not going to limit her contact with you to a phone call."

Alex added more brandy to their glasses. "I've noticed that people tend to become more stubborn as they age."

Boris nodded. "I think that's right." He sighed, drank, and added, "We usually know so little about other people. I don't even know how old my mother was. Did she ever tell you?"

"Yes, she said she was born in January of 1861."

"That means she was seventy-one, and was only twenty-one when I was born." He grinned suddenly. "My father was at least thirty years older than she, and you are almost that much younger. That must be some kind of record. What a woman!"

"I agree. She was quite a woman. I consider I was very fortunate to have had her as a wife."

Boris put his glass down and got to his feet. "Have you made any funeral arrangements yet?"

"Yes, it will be day after tomorrow. I assume you'll stay here. There is plenty of room and you are welcome."

"Thank you, but I've already arranged to stay with my old college roommate. I always do when I'm here, and he stays with me when he is in the U.S. May I use your phone? He's to pick me up."

"Of course," Alex said, relieved by that information. "It's on the desk just behind you."

After making his call, Boris asked, "Is there another title defense in the works?" It would be at least an hour before his friend could get there.

"Probably not. There's no sponsorship money floating around during this depression. There hasn't been a tournament of real consequence in more than a year. Prize money has dried up. Professional chess players have joined the ranks of the unemployed. How has the depression affected your university?"

"There has been a lot of belt-tightening. Having tenure, my job would appear safe, but money for research and other useful activities has gone into hiding. Also, enrollment of new students has dropped off. As a result, a number of non-tenured people have been let go, and those of us remaining have had to take on larger teaching loads. Considering the economic situation, I guess I shouldn't complain."

"Well, you're fortunate to have assured income. Even in good times, professional chess is a precarious business, and only the best can get by on chess earnings."

"Did winning the title make much of a difference for you?"

"Yes, a great one. Until the world economy collapsed, I was able to provide Nadyezhda with the kind of lifestyle she enjoyed, and still put something aside, which has come in handy the last couple of years."

Tactful, Boris stuck to the subject of chess, not mentioning the money he had continued to send his mother monthly, even after her marriage. "Our press continue to carry Capablanca's complaints about not getting a return match."

"I'm sure they do. I have a thick file of communications from him full of demands, accusations, complaints, insults, threats—you name it. What he doesn't mention is that he has never met the requirements specified for a match—regulations which he himself decreed in 1921, and which I had to meet. Now, he wants to change the rules, which he claims are unreasonable. To hell with that! When he is ready to comply with his own rules he can have his match. And when that happens, I'll beat him easily and quickly. It won't be like the last time. You can quote me on that to your press." Glowering, he tossed off what was left in his glass, opened a new bottle and poured more for each of them.

Boris was surprised at the number of people who were present at the funeral service.

"There's a large White Russian colony here," Alex explained, "and she was acquainted with many of them."

Not many of the chess-playing fraternity had met Nadyezhda, but a considerable number of them also came out of respect for Alex.

"I trust we'll see each other the next time you are on our side of the Atlantic," Boris said, when they were parting.

"I'll certainly try to arrange it," Alex replied. Neither had any illusions that another meeting would be anything other than accidental.

Alex felt a genuine sense of loss. His marriage had not been for love, but Nadyezhda had turned it into a success by making his comfort and welfare her first order of business, and she had also learned quickly how to cater to his various moods. She rarely complained about anything.

"I wish you were sailing back with us," Nadyezhda had told Lupi, when they were leaving Buenos Aires after the match.

"I wish I were, too, but the business we have been developing here has been so good that I've been ordered to stay on for another month."

"If that's the case, your company owes me a share of the profits, since you only came here because of me!" Alex said, laughing.

"That's not what I told them when I recommended exploring the Argentinean market. Besides, you said you couldn't do it without my help. Let's say we're even, partner."

"Gladly, partner, since I got the best of the deal."

The "All Ashore" whistle warned Lupi to leave the ship. Nadyezhda hugged and kissed him. Alex also embraced him, and they stood at the rail, waving to him until the ship pulled away.

"What a wonderful man!" she said. "How lucky you are to have him for a friend."

Back in Paris, Alex received a hero's welcome from the White Russian population, as well as from the chess community. Editorials praising his victory appeared in several newspapers, and the Paris governing council presented him with a special citation.

After basking in this sunshine for a few months and getting some replacements for lost teeth, the Alekhines set out on a six-month, lucrative, global tour. Nadyezhda's main task during that period was to keep his consumption of wine and spirits within reasonable limit—not always easy to do, considering the convivial reception accorded them everywhere, and his natural inclinations.

He and Lupi wrote to each other frequently. Late in 1928 Alex sent a note to him.

I shall be defending my crown in September against Boguljubov. Would you be willing to serve as my second again? I can guarantee that it won't be another drawn-out affair. I know his game well. There won't be many draws. The match is to be in Wiesbaden. While your transportation expense is not included, the sponsors will take care of your living expenses. Nadyezhda joins me in hoping you will be there to give us the benefit of your sage advice and diplomatic talents, as well as the pleasure of your company.

Lupi was there, they all enjoyed themselves, and Alex won the match easily.

Unlike Capablanca, Alex made it a point to take part in as many major European tournaments as possible. These he dominated, rarely losing a game, and not even yielding many draws. The style of play he had used to win the championship was put aside. His games sparkled, and his preeminence was acknowledged by everyone, except for Capablanca and his adherents.

Nadyezhda's unexpected death brought the most contented seven years of Alex's life to an abrupt end. He was alone again.

Twenty-one

It was the largest book store in Paris but, as the clerk pointed out, they had no demand to stock a Portuguese-English dictionary. If it would help, they could sell her a volume for translating Portuguese into French and another for going from French to English, but Grace Wishart shook her head in frustration. She turned to her companion and, in her Midwestern accent, said, "It's hopeless. I'll never get it straight in time."

Alex, waiting behind them with a volume he had found reporting the games of a recent American tournament, said, "Pardon me, but I heard what you were asking for. Perhaps I can be of assistance."

Both women turned in surprise. "Oh," Grace answered, "someone who speaks English. You aren't American, though, are you?"

"No, but I do speak English, and as it happens, I also speak Portuguese. Is there something which needs translating?"

"Yes, a document full of legal language which I can't understand."

Alex smiled and, handing her his card, said, "That should not be a problem. As you can see, I happen to hold a degree in law and, I might add, earned my living for a number of years in Portugal as a translator of foreign languages."

"It's a miracle, Grace!" the other woman exclaimed, "It's just what you want."

"Maybe," said Grace. She had never put much stock in miracles.

"As soon as I pay for this book," he said, "I shall be happy to try to help you with your problem. That is, of course, if you wish."

"Of course she'll welcome whatever help you can give, won't you, Grace?"

"Yes, if you really can."

132

After paying the clerk, he suggested, "Perhaps we might visit the café next door and have some coffee while you explain the nature of your problem."

"All right. My name is Grace Wishart," she said, offering her hand, "and this is my friend, Dorothy Jackson."

Alex shook hands with each of them, then held the door open.

It was mid-afternoon, so they had their choice of tables in the café. After they had ordered, Grace said, "I am an American, but am living a few miles from Paris in a house which my husband left me. He passed away four months ago. He was a mining engineer, and sometimes made investments in other countries where his work took him. One was as a partner in a company in Brazil. I recently received a letter from them saying that they were in the process of selling the company, and wanted my signature on some documents. These are all in Portuguese. My knowledge of that language is very limited, but from what I can make out, it seems to me they are not offering a fair amount for my husband's interests. In the letter, which is in English, they say that the sale is to be completed at the end of the month, regardless of whether they receive my signatures. I'm afraid they are trying to pressure me, but unless I fully understand the meaning of the documents, I don't know what to do."

"Do you have the papers with you?"

"No, they are at the house."

"Well, I can't advise you without seeing them, but if your suspicions arc justified, it may be possible to stop the sale until the questions are properly answered. I have a friend in Rio de Janeiro who is an attorney, and I believe a cable to him could hold up the process for awhile."

"That's just what's needed," said Dorothy.

"Yes," Grace agreed, still wary of this urbane stranger, but swallowing her doubts. "Would you be able to look at the papers tomorrow if I bring them in?"

"Yes, I'll be happy to."

"Where shall we meet? At your office?"

"That will be fine." He wrote the address on another card. "I have my office at my apartment, since much of my time is spent out of the country."

"Is so much of your practice in foreign countries?" Dorothy asked.

"I am not actively carrying on a law practice at the present, but am continuing the career of a professional chess player, a field in which I have the honor to hold the world championship."

"Really?" she said, astonished.

Grace stared at him, her eyebrows and doubts both raised, "If you aren't practicing...?"

"Let me reassure you. I would be examining the documents primarily to translate them for you. After they are clear you can decide on a course of action. If it seems indicated, and you agree, we could cable the necessary information to the lawyer. In any case, I would not be representing you, and there would be no charge for my services. I just wish to be helpful, if I can."

Grace saw Dorothy's encouraging nod, and said, "Would two o'clock be satisfactory?"

"Two o'clock will be fine."

Starting to fasten her full-length mink coat as she stood, Grace said, "Okay, we'll see you then."

"What an unusual man," Dorothy observed, after they had left him. "A professional chess champion! Can you imagine that?"

"I didn't know there was such a thing. I know nothing about chess, except that I once saw my grandfather playing with another old man, and that was at least fifty years ago."

"My brothers used to play, but their games usually ended in arguments about one of them cheating. I think they made their own rules."

"You'll come along with me tomorrow, won't you?" Grace asked.

"Of course. That man interests me."

"Don't be silly! He's at least ten years younger than you."

"So what? I can dream, can't I? I hope I still can when I get to be your age. Wouldn't you like to find another man?"

"Not especially. Thirty-five years of marriage was enough for me!"

"Having had two husbands, I know that there's something to be said for variety. Life with an attorney and a linguist, who also travels the world as chess champion, might be an interesting experience," Dorothy responded.

"I just hope he is what he claims. Someone with all those qualifications showing up out of the blue is something I'm still finding hard to swallow."

134

"You shouldn't be so suspicious. How was he to know that we'd be coming into that store? I'm sure it was just a lucky accident. Anyway, as long as you don't sign anything unless you understand it, you should be safe. Besides, I'll be there as a witness."

Alex scanned the half-dozen items, then read each aloud in Portuguese—translating each sentence as he finished it. He followed this with a discussion of what he considered to be the legal questions involved.

"You were right," he told Grace, "to question the proposal the company offered. You are definitely entitled to a much better settlement. If you wish to retain him, we can draft a cable for you to send to the attorney in Rio whom I mentioned. I am confident he can handle the matter to your satisfaction. The issues are quite straightforward."

Grace glanced at Dorothy for guidance, then said, "Very well. I guess the sooner the better."

"Definitely. Time is running out."

After it was out of the way, he suggested refreshments. "All I can offer, I'm sorry to say, is coffee, tea or brandy. Since the recent loss of my wife, I have kept very little food at home."

"Thank you, but we don't want to put you to any trouble..."

Dorothy broke in at that point, saying, "That's right. A little brandy would be the simplest, wouldn't it, Grace?"

"I suppose so."

"Fine," he said, "I'll be right back."

While he was out of the room, Dorothy walked around to examine the dozens of cups, plaques, citations, and other awards covering the fireplace mantel and bookshelves. "He wasn't kidding about being champion. Here's the proof."

Grace glanced around without much interest. "Yes, I suppose."

"Your trophy collection is most impressive," Dorothy said, as he entered, carrying a tray with a decanter and glasses. "How many do you have?"

"I have no idea. Many which I received in my younger days were lost when our home in Moscow was destroyed by the Bolsheviks."

"You are Russian?" asked Grace.

"Yes, but after the war I left Russia, and am now a citizen of France."

"Obviously then you know Russian, as well as French, Portuguese and English," said Dorothy. "What others do you speak?"

"German, Italian and Spanish quite well, and a little Swedish, plus a smattering of maybe a half-dozen Asian languages, which I picked up on my travels."

"How much traveling do you do?"

"During the last ten years, I suppose I have been on the road at least half the time. Most of that involved tournaments or matches in Europe, the United States, or South America. After winning the world championship four years ago, my wife and I made a round-the-world trip, which included exhibitions in the Philippines, China, Australia and India, along with stops in a few other countries."

"That sounds fascinating. I'd love to see some of those exotic places. Wouldn't you, Grace?"

"Not particularly. The U.S. and France have enough to satisfy me. I can do without unnecessary travel. I had my fill of it when Joe insisted I go with him, and it isn't much fun when you don't understand what people are saying." She finished the brandy in her glass.

"It can be frustrating, if you do not know the language," he said, rising to offer her a refill.

"No more, thank you. I think we really should be going. I do thank you very much for your help, and will let you know when I get an answer to the cable."

"Fine. I'll be interested to know what happens. I'm confident the news will be good."

Grace Wishart telephoned a few days later to inform him that she had received a cable from the Brazilian attorney accepting the case. She called sometime later with the news that she had received a revised offer from the company, with apparently far more acceptable terms. She had some new documents requiring her signature, and would appreciate his examining and confirming her interpretation of them before accepting the offer. They arranged to meet at his apartment at eleven the next morning.

"Yes," Alex said, after reading all of the papers she had brought, "everything looks in order, and this appears to be a more equitable payment for your interests. My friend obviously made it clear to them that they could not take advantage of you."

136

"Yes, and I am very grateful to you for helping me to get his services. This offer is more than twice the original one. I know you said you wanted no payment for your assistance, but..."

"No," he interrupted, "I meant it, and am happy that it turned out so well."

"In that case," said Dorothy Jackson, who had come again with Grace, "at least, this calls for some kind of celebration, doesn't it, Grace?"

"Yes. If nothing else, you will let us take you to lunch, won't you?"

He smiled. "Gladly. It will be a privilege. It has been a long time since I've had the pleasure of feminine companionship at a meal."

During lunch, which included a celebratory bottle of champagne, Grace said, "With this out of the way, I'm returning to New York next month to wind up some other matters."

"But you will be coming back here?"

"Yes, I plan to spend most of my time here from now on. I expect to be gone only five or six weeks."

"Are you also going?" he asked Dorothy.

"No. I'll stay here and spend a few days each week at Grace's place, keeping an eye on the hired help. The rest of the time I'll be at a small apartment I have here in Paris." Her brief, arch look as she spoke was unmistakable.

"In that case," he said, "I hope I may prevail on you to accompany me to the theater or opera some evening?"

"I'd love to," she said, her smile almost turning into a smirk as she caught a glimpse of Grace's raised eyebrows.

"You're a shameless cradle snatcher," said Grace, as soon as Alex had left "throwing yourself at him like that!"

"What do you mean? What's wrong with accepting a chance to go to the opera? And a widower in his forties left the cradle long ago. I've been out with men younger than Alex, and they never complained about my age."

"I just hope you know what you're doing. I'm grateful for the help he gave me, but there is something about that man that leaves me uneasy."

"Oh, Grace, you're such a fuddy-duddy! He's a perfect gentleman. I've never seen such nice manners."

"Maybe he's too perfect. Just watch your step."

"Don't worry. My two husbands taught me well."

Twenty-two

Within a week after Grace sailed for New York, Alex and Dorothy dined and went to the theater. They returned to her apartment, had a few drinks and, to neither's surprise and with mutual satisfaction, spent the remainder of the night in her bed.

At one point, during a respite for a cigarette, Dorothy sighed with pleasure and said, "If either of my husbands had known how to treat a woman the way you do, I would have put up with their other faults. Your wife was a lucky woman."

"The luck wasn't all hers. I learned a lot from her, too."

"Was it your first marriage?"

"It was my first, but her third. She was twice widowed."

"Really? And you were married seven years? She must have been older than you."

"Yes, by thirty years."

"Thirty! You're joking."

"No, it's true. The age difference didn't matter. She was intelligent, interesting, and full of vitality. That's what is important. Years mean nothing."

"You give me hope. I've been bothered, because I think I'm a few years older than you. Most mature men only seem interested in girls barely out of their teens."

"Those men really aren't mature. If they were, they would have better judgment. As for you, you are clearly a self-reliant person, living the way you wish. If you want to marry again, I'm sure you will have no trouble finding suitors."

"I am able to get by better on my own, certainly, than Grace. Having to make decisions is something new for her. Joe Wishart always took care of everything, but while he knew how to make a lot of money, he never thought of preparing her to manage if anything happened to him. I guess he thought he was immortal."

Alex put out his cigarette, and began rubbing the nape of her neck. "The Brazilian company wasn't her only concern?"

"Lord, no! Joe had holdings in all kinds of things; mines, farms, stocks, you name it. The depression has hit some of them, but she's still a rich woman. I can get along comfortably with what I have, and managing it is no problem for me, but it's nothing like what she'll have to deal with, and with no experience."

She took a last puff, dropped her cigarette in the ashtray, turned to him, blew gently in his ear, and said, "But that's not our headache, is it?"

"No, it's not," he murmured, kissing her throat, then moving down to her breasts.

"When will you be back?" Dorothy asked.

"Not for seven weeks."

"I'm going to miss this," she said, stroking his calf with her toes.

"Not as much as I shall, but my bank account needs an infusion."

"Will you earn much?"

"I expect to make this trip worthwhile. I should win first prize in all three tournaments. Since they depend on my presence to draw spectators, I receive an extra fee just for participating, as well as my travel expenses. I'll also earn money from some exhibitions, and will be paid for preparing annotated analyses later of all of the games from two of the tournaments. That will keep me busy for some time after I return."

"What an unusual way to earn a living! I wish I were going with you. I've been to Madrid, but I've never seen Granada."

"There's a lot to see there, but I wouldn't have time to be with you. When I'm playing, I'm busy late at night studying adjourned games."

"Where else do you go?"

"Lisbon. I'll be there for twelve days before coming home. Then we can have more of these wonderful nights."

"It won't be so easy. Grace gets back in a few weeks."

"Don't worry. I'm sure we can find some way to keep that from being a problem."

Alex walked out of the Palace Hotel in Madrid just as the doorman was opening a taxi door. He was about to ask the man to hold the cab for him, when his eyes met those of the woman just emerging. Even with a lapse of twenty years, each of them instantly recognized the other. He was about to speak, but Rosa Pereira, her eyes widening in horror, jumped back into the vehicle, which pulled away as she slammed the door.

Surprised, the doorman stood there with his hand outstretched, as though waiting for a tip. Alex shuddered, as though an icy wind had struck him. Long-buried memories of Rosa and Maria rose in his mind. After an unsettled evening, Alex finally drifted into a fitful sleep...

> *He is walking beside a canal in Venice. Hearing a violin, he turns and sees Rosa standing in a gondola playing Song of the Volga Boatman. He calls to her, but she ignores him and the gondola disappears in the distance.*

He ground his teeth as he slept, but did not awaken.

Twenty-three

Alex returned from the kitchen after washing the mud off his hand. His door key had slipped out of his hand and bounced from the step into the flower bed next to the front door. He hung his dripping coat and hat on the hall tree, walked into the parlor and poured himself a drink.

"Any mail?" he asked, after wolfing down the brandy.

"On the dining room table," said Grace, not bothering to look up from her book.

He added some more brandy to his glass and went into the dining room, where he sat down and separated the letters from several chess journals which had arrived. Using his penknife he slit open the four envelopes. The first letter was from someone suggesting a different seventeenth move which he was sure would have given Alex a win instead of just a draw in a recent tournament game. His brow furrowed for a few seconds, then he grinned and tossed the letter aside. He would show the writer how such a move would have been catastrophic for him, and would have lost the game. Next was an inquiry as to his fee for giving an exhibition at a chess club in Lyon. The third letter was from Antonio Lupi, telling him that plans were under way for another tournament in Lisbon, and inviting Alex to stay with him if he decided to participate.

The remaining letter bore an Amsterdam postmark. After reading the letter, Alex returned to the parlor with it and his glass. He refilled the glass, sat down, lit a cigarette, and blew smoke at Grace to get her attention.

She scowled. "Did you have to do that?"

Ignoring her words, he said, "I've just received an interesting challenge for a title match."

"Who is it from?"

"Euwe."

"Euwe? What a strange name. Who is he?"

"The Dutch champion. A good player, for an amateur. He's a mathematics professor."

"Will you accept?"

"Sure. He won't give me any trouble. I've already beaten him in a short match, and know how he plays. There's a $10,000 purse, and the money will come in handy."

"That's for certain! Your sure-thing stock investments are making us poorer by the hour."

He swallowed the last of his drink, glaring at her. "You never stop, do you? Those stocks will make us a fortune. The companies are just having to adjust to meet the depression conditions."

"I doubt those companies will still be around by the time this depression ends."

"Just wait. I know what I'm doing."

Watching him pour still more from the decanter, she said, "You won't know which end is up, if you keep swilling that stuff."

"Don't you worry your pretty little head. I know how much I can handle." Only a few drops spilled when his shoulder brushed the door frame as he stalked from the room.

At breakfast the next morning, she brought up the proposed match. "After your win again last year against Boguljubov, weren't you committed to play Nimzovich or Capablanca next?"

"Nimzovich will keep. As for Capablanca, fuck him! I don't owe him anything. He can rot in hell, for all I care!"

"Where would this match with Euwe—is that right?—be played?"

"The sponsors are some Dutch manufacturers, and they suggest that the games be played in a series of towns in Holland. They believe that would help boost overall attendance."

"Is that arrangement okay with you?"

"Sure. Distances there are short, and I don't care where we play."

"When is it supposed to begin?"

"That's just one of many details still to be worked out. As far as I'm concerned, it can be soon. I won't need much time to get ready for him."

"Don't expect me to go along with you this time. I was bored stiff during your last match, and I certainly don't relish the idea of moving around constantly from one hotel to another."

"That's okay with me. I won't have to worry about your entertainment. We're each allowed to have a second for the match, and I'll try to get Lupi again for the job."

Play began in Zandvoort. On October 19, 1935, Alex celebrated his forty-third birthday with a win, giving him a 6–3 lead in points. The winner would be the first to collect 15½ points, draws counting in this match as half-points for each player. In the remote event of a tie score after thirty games, Alex would retain the title.

Well-organized, imperturbable, Max Euwe, age thirty-four, had no intention of making adjustments to his game plan. He knew he couldn't match the brilliance of the champion. He had told a reporter that Alex was capable of converting an apparently lifeless position into a master piece of art, when no one else would see enough in it to justify a picture postcard. Even so, he remained cool and confident that his scientific approach to chess was worth more, over a long match, than brilliance, and that superior physical stamina would count in the end. Despite his teaching responsibilities, he had always kept himself in excellent condition, with a regular schedule of swimming and boxing.

"An interesting game," Antonio Lupi observed, as they sat in Alex's hotel room. He was still nursing his first post-game brandy, while Alex was pouring his third.

"Yes," Alex replied, with a big grin. "Actually, he had enough of an edge early in the game to win it, but he doesn't have the killer instinct. I got a reprieve."

"It was really something, the way you turned the game around with the rook sacrifice. Coming out of the blue like that threw him for a loop."

Alex laughed, and emptied his glass.

His friend was struck by Alex's mood as they were having dinner following the next game. It had been a draw, one that had stretched over eighty moves and required two full days. "You're that much closer to clinching the match," he said, in an effort to inject a cheerful note.

"That's not the point," Alex replied. "I had two good chances to put him away, and I overlooked them both. Inexcusable." They had finished one bottle of wine and he had told the waiter to bring another.

"I think a night out might be a good thing, since there's no game tomorrow. Why don't we visit a nightclub?"

"No, I want to review just how I managed to botch today's game. Maybe we'll relax tomorrow night."

"Take my advice, Alex, and leave it until tomorrow when you'll be rested. I believe you are more tired than you think."

Alex gazed at Lupi's earnest face and gave in. "Okay, maybe you're right. Where should we go?"

Lupi saw the waiter approaching with the wine. "Let's ask him."

❖ ❖ ❖

Still droopy-eyed at dusk, Lupi watched Alex frowning at the board. "I'm sorry, but I think I'd better have a short nap before dinner." Lupi had slept restlessly after their night out, which had lasted too long.

"Okay. If I'm not here when you are ready to eat, I'll be in the bar," Alex replied.

The short nap extended two hours longer than Lupi had planned. Not finding Alex at the bar, he tried the dining room without success. He went back to the bar to ask if Alex had been there.

"Yes, he was here for quite awhile."

"He left no message?"

"No. He did say he thought he'd get some fresh air. He looked as though he could use some."

The path from the building to the highway was the only illuminated part of the now dark grounds, and Lupi followed it. Shortly before reaching the road, he heard a moan. In a ditch a few feet to his left, Alex lay retching.

A hotel employee helped Lupi raise Alex out of a pool of vomit, take him through a rear door of the hotel, and up to his room via a service elevator. Together they removed his vomit-stained jacket, his urine-soaked trousers and underwear, and put him to bed, where he immediately began sonorous snoring.

After tipping the employee generously and extracting a promise of silence about the episode, Lupi tracked down both the match director and Euwe. He told them that Alex was experiencing an intestinal upset and would be unable to compete the following day. Both men were concerned and offered to get medical help, but Lupi said Alex told him that shouldn't be needed, and that he was confident that only a one-day postponement of competition would be required.

While shaving the following morning, the telephone interrupted Lupi.

"Antonio? I don't think I'll be able to play today."

"I was sure you couldn't. I've already gotten a postponement until tomorrow. How do you feel?"

"I've been better. Maybe a bath will help."

"I imagine it will. I'll be by to see you in about an hour."

"What happened last night? Did I disgrace myself?"

"I'll tell you when I get there. Consider yourself lucky that your performance was kept from public notice."

"That must have been your doing. Thanks. I owe you."

Lupi watched with troubled eyes the next day as Alex labored over the board. The bold, imaginative ideas, so characteristic of his play, were missing and he soon found himself in an awkward constricted position. After a fruitless search for relief, the flag on his clock fell. The loss brought Euwe within two points of a win.

Twenty-four

"Ready for dinner, Alex?"

"No, I'm not going down. I'll order something from room service."

"Be sure you do," Lupi said, aware of the ever-present tumbler of brandy in Alex's hand. "Some solid food would do you good."

"I will. Don't worry."

"Should I come back later to review the game with you?"

"Not tonight. I think I'll turn in early."

"Good idea. See you at breakfast at the usual time."

Alex was in no mood for one of Lupi's pep talks. Slumped in a chair, he swirled the brandy in his glass, agonizing. Two games in a row! He couldn't believe he had lost consecutive games. Suddenly, after twenty-four games, the score was tied. What was going on? Why? Why couldn't he settle down? He hadn't felt this edgy even during the darkest moments of his match with Capablanca—even through the ordeal with his teeth. What had made it possible then for him to keep his concentration, his confidence? Nothing was different, except that in Buenos Aires Nadyezhda was always there as a stabilizer, anticipating his needs, comforting him in bed, always in the right place with the right words. She helped him focus his energies, and be able to stick to the demanding task of playing in a style completely foreign to his natural instincts, a style essential to beating the arrogant Cuban—an opponent far more formidable than Euwe.

Where was the support he needed now? Staring into the half-empty tumbler he saw the image of Nadyezhda's face transform into Grace's. With all his strength, he slung the glass across the room, where it shattered against the wall, spattering furniture, clothing and rugs with its contents.

146

Winning the twenty-fifth game, Euwe took the lead for the first time in the match. Alex used his last postponement to try to stop the hemorrhaging, but was unsuccessful. The Dutch champion won the twenty-sixth game — his fourth in succession! — leaving Alex in an almost helpless position. Desperate, he opened the next game with moves he had not used in eight years. The gamble paid off. With three games left, he was only one point behind. Unruffled, Euwe calmly obtained draws in the next two games. With the score now 15–14, Alex had to win the final game to retain his title.

A capacity crowd of two thousand observers crowded into Bellevue Hall in Amsterdam that evening for the contest. After almost five hours, his head shaking in frustration, Alex stumbled to his feet, conceded that the game was a draw, and shook Euwe's hand.

Their emotions showing — Euwe's for the first time — the two men stood, arms around each other, as photographers' flashbulbs blazed, and the partisan crowd cheered for the new champion.

Twenty-five

How could she have done it? She'd had doubts about him from the moment she first saw him. She had even warned Dorothy that this smooth-talking stranger wasn't just what he seemed, even though he had come through when they first met with the help she had so desperately needed. In addition, he was helpful in several other matters after her return from New York, so her reservations gradually faded away. Obligated, she couldn't refuse an invitation to attend the opera with him. The evening turned out so enjoyable that she accepted other invitations, and soon found herself looking forward to his attentive company. Inevitably, after too much champagne one evening, this led to a few hours in bed, unlike any she had ever known during the many years with Joe. The next thing she knew, she was married to this man!

At first, she persuaded herself that she had gained a partner who could relieve her from the burdens of investment decisions—where she had little confidence in her own abilities—leaving her free to concentrate on management of the farm. That was something she enjoyed.

What she had done, though, was turn her resources over to a man with a gambler's mentality, whose judgment was not helped—as she discovered only after they were married—by his generous consumption of alcohol. In a year the value of her stock holdings had gone down almost twenty percent. Now, with the loss of the chess championship, his own earning potential would also decline.

To top it off, no longer could she call on Dorothy for her advice. She had been astounded at how Dorothy had exploded when she learned of their marriage. It was only then that Dorothy's expectations to marry Alex came to light. After that, Dorothy had disappeared from their lives.

Now there was no one but Alex to help her, and he hadn't drawn a sober breath since losing to Euwe.

Lupi fully appreciated the impact which loss of the title would have on Alex. Like the little Dutch boy, he tried to put his finger in the dike. At the end of the match, he said, "Euwe may wear the crown, Alex, but everyone knows that you are still the finest player in the world."

"Bullshit! Now I'll just be considered another has-been."

"That's not true, and you can prove it by beating Max in a return match."

"What makes you think there will be one? He won't dare give me another chance."

"I believe he is a man of his word, and will give you the first crack at the next match. And, if you train properly and get yourself in shape, you have what it takes."

"I suppose you mean that I drink too much."

"Alex, no one should know better than you the physical and mental demands of a championship match. The truth is, you were not in proper shape, either at the start or as it went on, to do what had to be done."

Alex slammed his glass down on the table, walked to the door of his hotel room, opened it, and said, "Antonio, thank you for your advice, but I can do without any more of your moralizing!"

Stone-faced, Lupi walked out of the room without another word.

Alex turned to the nearest wall and hit it, breaking both the plaster and his hand.

If there had been only one reporter present, it probably would have been defined as an interview. Since someone from a second paper also came, it was called a press conference. Anyone else showing up would have had to stand. There was only room for two chairs in Max Euwe's office at the university. Behind his desk he sat erect awaiting the inevitable question.

"When can we expect a defense of your title?"

"In 1937, just as I said, when I won it last year."

"Is it true that Capablanca has challenged you to a match?"

"Yes. I heard from him last week."

"Will you accept it?"

"Capablanca certainly deserves a chance to regain the title and, in my opinion, should have had that opportunity years ago. Before accepting his challenge, however, I feel honor-bound to learn whether Dr. Alekhine wishes a return match, since I had given him my word that he could have the first chance. Consequently, I wrote to him just yesterday to renew my offer."

"Which one would you prefer to play?"

"I have no preference. Both of them rank among the greatest players in history. I feel fortunate to hold the title while they are still active."

"Is Alekhine still competing? I haven't seen his name among the participants in tournaments for quite awhile."

"I don't know. That is why I have written to him."

A fragment of a smile settled on Alex's mouth for an instant. It had been a year since anything like that had appeared. He re-read the letter, then went outdoors and walked completely around the château twice, wrestling with a decision.

He went back inside, packed a bag, and came downstairs.

"Going somewhere?" Grace asked, looking up.

"Yes, to Lisbon. I'm not sure when I'll be back."

She shrugged, and returned to her book.

He telephoned for a taxi and went outside to wait.

Twenty-six

"Could I come see you?"

Surprised by the familiar voice, Lupi said, "Is there any reason why you should?"

"Yes. I want to apologize."

Alex held his breath during the eternity which followed, exhaling only when the answer came.

"Where are you?"

"At the rail station."

"Very well. Be at my office in an hour."

"I'll be there. And, thank you."

"Sit down, Alex." The bloodshot haunted eyes, the sagging jowls, the overall air of decline shocked him. The man had aged by at least ten years.

Alex fumbled for a cigarette, lit it with a shaking hand. His voice was low when he finally spoke. "Antonio, this is a new experience for me. This is the first time in my life that I have ever apologized to anyone for anything. No matter how I felt, what I said to you last year was inexcusable. Much of the success I've had in the past wouldn't have happened without your advice and support. My performance in the match with Euwe would have been even worse than it was, except for you, and I shudder to think what would have happened to my reputation if it weren't for your efforts. I ask your forgiveness."

Lupi looked at him. This was an Alekhine he had never seen, one he would never have imagined, a man on the verge of collapse. "Your words did hurt me, Alex, a lot. I know, though, what losing the match meant to you. I am willing to forget what happened." Seeing tears gathering in the other man's eyes, he said, "What have you been doing since?"

Alex took a final puff, stubbed out his cigarette in an ashtray, shook his head, and said, "Drinking. That's all, just drinking."

The blunt admission surprised him even more than the abject apology he had received. How Alex could consume brandy like water while still producing such chess masterpieces was something he could never understand, but he had known that no one could do so indefinitely. More than once as his second in title matches he had offered carefully worded suggestions that Alex restrain himself. Invariably, his words were ignored. Admitting now to his drinking problem demonstrated the depth of his desperation. "What about chess?"

His face contorted, he lit another cigarette before answering. "Lupi, only three people have ever really known me. My mother, of course. Nadyezhda, who probably understood me better than anyone. You are the third one, and you can probably look at me more objectively, because love isn't involved." He puffed furiously a few times before continuing. "Except, I guess I should say, for love of chess. That's what motivated you when you talked me out of returning to Russia more than twenty years ago."

True, Lupi thought to himself, though he'd always suspected the times being what they were then, Alex hadn't required much persuasion. It was evident that he welcomed an excuse to remain in Lisbon.

"It has never been a secret that I've always believed I was the best chess player alive. The possibility of losing—for any reason whatsoever—was something I refused to consider. You knew better. You knew it would happen, and you knew why it would happen. The reason was clear and simple. Booze. Too much booze."

Lupi nodded.

"During the match, I know you tried to get me to exercise greater self-control, but it was too late. If Nadyezhda had still been alive, she would have been able to speak more forcefully, and I believe would have kept me from self-destruction. She was always there when I needed her—something which can't be said for Grace, though that's no excuse for my not being able to stand on my own feet." He drew on the cigarette, then put it down as he began coughing uncontrollably.

Lupi poured some water from a carafe on his desk and Alex drank until the coughing stopped.

"Thanks. When I got home, I should have faced up to the truth, but I didn't. Instead of planning how to regain the title, I just sat around feeling sorry for myself. For a year, all I've done is drink. I've been my own worst enemy." He grimaced, stood up, took a few steps, sat down again. "Now, suddenly, I have a chance for redemption. Max Euwe, a true gentleman, wrote to me. He has received a challenge from Capa, which he is willing to accept, but says I am entitled to a return-match first, if I want one. If I want one? That's all in life I do want! But I will have no chance of winning unless I can turn myself around. That is why I am here. I've become weak. I can't do it without your help. There is no one else."

Lupi sat dumbfounded. This was not the first time Alex had asked for his help. He had served as his second four times. But this self-abasement was something he had never before encountered. Here was a man—ever proud, self-confident, even arrogant—humbling himself, pleading to be rescued from self-destruction.

After a long pause, he asked, "Do you have Max's letter with you?"

"Yes." Alex took an envelope from his breast pocket and handed it to him.

"I see that he suggests beginning play in September," Lupi said, after reading the letter, "which leaves only four months. Tell me, when did you have your last drink?"

"At the station, just after I phoned. I needed one to be able to face you," he confessed.

Torn between doubt and a residual sense of obligation, Lupi debated his answer. Was there time to rebuild this wreck, assuming its materials could be salvaged? Should he try? How? "If I try to do what you ask, how soon could we start?"

"Today, right now!" Alex replied, gulping.

"Do you need to return to Paris?"

"No."

"Do you have anything to drink with you?"

Alex removed a silver flask from a side pocket of his jacket, and placed it on the desk.

"Any more in your bag?"

Sheepishly, Alex opened his suitcase and took out two bottles of brandy.

Lupi rose, walked over to where Alex stood. His eyes burned a path to the taller man. "Here are my conditions. First of all, you have already had your last taste of anything alcoholic, anything—wine, beer, vodka, gin, brandy, whatever—until after the match has ended. Is that clear?"

His voice shaking, Alex muttered, "Yes, I understand."

"I hope you do, because if you have even one drink, the deal is off, and I am through with you forever. Is that clear?"

Alex nodded agreement.

"Next, we have a small vineyard near here which is not in production this year. There is no one there at present except for a caretaker and his wife. I will take you to a small cottage tomorrow where you can stay on the grounds until time for the match. Your primary duty will be to restore yourself physically—doing calisthenics, walking, chopping wood, helping the caretaker with chores. I will furnish you with exercise equipment, such as dumbbells and Indian clubs. You must spend four hours every day on such activities. The rest of the time you can use for chess. I still have all of Euwe's games which we had collected before the first match—but which you didn't bother to review—and you can work with those. I will spend as much time there with you as I can spare. Do you agree to follow that program completely?"

"Yes, absolutely. I will do just as you say. That's a promise," Alex said, his eyes filling.

Lupi held out his hand, and Alex held onto it with both of his.

"Oh, yes. One more detail. You will have all of your meals with the caretaker, and I will instruct his wife as to your diet."

Alex threw his arms around him. "Thank you, Antonio. I trust your judgment completely."

> *"Three spades," Capablanca declares.*
> *Caroline Marshall answers, "Three no-trump."*
> *Nadyezhda doesn't hesitate. "Seven spades."*
> *Lupi roars with laughter. "You don't have any more chance of making seven spades than Alex has of beating Max Euwe! I double."*
> *Furious at hearing that, Alex takes another swig of vodka.*

*The melody Rosa was playing in the background
abruptly swells to deafening volume, causing the bottle to
shatter in his hand.*
  "I knew you couldn't keep your word," Lupi sneers.
  *Alex throws himself down in the mud, weeping in frus-
tration.*

He awoke with a jerk, his body covered in sweat. The craving for a drink had kept him awake for hours. Whenever he did drop off, his sleep was interrupted by the plaintive cry of a violin. At last, he surrendered and paced the floor until it was time for Lupi to pick him up.

It was a simple, box-like, gray stucco structure, its dullness relieved only by the alternating blue and green tiles outlining the door and single front window. Alicia Delgado, the caretaker's wife, unlocked the door, handed Alex the key, and waited while he and Lupi made a brief tour of the cottage. The three of them then walked the hundred feet to where she and her husband lived in a slightly larger house. Pedro Delgado put down the sledgehammer he was using to drive in a replacement fence post and joined them in the kitchen.

Lupi made no effort to spare Alex embarrassment as he issued his instructions. He concluded by telling them, "If I learn that either of you has given Alex a single drink of even wine, you will be looking for new jobs."

The taciturn couple, both in their sixties, acknowledged him.

It wasn't easy, but by the time ten days had passed, the driving need for alcohol had faded. His eyes were starting to clear, and he no longer needed to stop for breath while climbing the low hill behind his cottage.

Lupi visited a few days later. He stopped first to question Alicia Delgado. "How's our patient doing?"

"You'll have to decide for yourself. I think he looks much better."

Lupi agreed. "You're beginning to look more like your old self, Alex. How do you feel?"

"Better, much better, thanks to you. I think your prescription is going to work."

"Is it still hard, doing without alcohol?"

"Yes. It's particularly bad watching the Delgados having wine with their meals. But I've resisted asking for any, remembering your threat to fire them if they gave me a drop."

Lupi smiled. "They've been around long enough to know that orders are meant to be followed."

"Have you always worked at this vineyard for the Lupis?" Alex asked Pedro.

"No. I worked at their biggest one for more than thirty years. They moved us here three years ago as a reward, letting us retire here, doing only as much work as we want."

"So Antonio's threat to fire you if I had a drink wasn't serious?"

Alicia snorted. "Ha! I've worked for the Lupis since before Tony was born. One of my first jobs was changing his diapers. He doesn't scare me." She looked at him, suspicion in her eyes. "You wouldn't be hinting for one, would you?"

"No, oh, no! I was just curious."

"That's good, because we wouldn't give you one. Anyone could see that you were sick when you got here, and why. Tony was right. You feel better already, don't you?"

"Yes. He was completely right. I am better, but I still have to recover even more in the next few months. I have important things to do."

It was the longest conversation the three of them would have during his stay at the vineyard.

Alex waited a month before advising Grace of his whereabouts. "I am undergoing physical and mental rehabilitation in preparation for a return match with Euwe in September," he wrote. "Believe it or not, I have not had a drop of alcohol in any form for the last thirty days, and won't until after the match. I intend to return home again holding the title of World Champion. I trust you have been managing, as I know you've had to for the past year, without any help from me."

Lupi was gratified, as he watched the progress Alex was making. He began to spend more and more time at the cottage, testing new concepts Alex was developing for possible use in the match. A month before it was to begin, he was convinced that Alex would regain the title, and told him so. "But, I shall not be going there with you. This time you will have to do it without my help."

Alex accepted that without argument. Lupi had been of great help in his previous matches, and he would have welcomed his support in this one. He knew, as well, that he would not have been able to play Euwe again if weren't for Lupi. He was aware, however, that he would not have the right to ever ask Lupi for any kind of help in the future.

As the date approached, the world chess community was in agreement that Euwe would win again, probably more easily than the first time. Though his whereabouts in recent months were unknown, rumors had spread that Alekhine had passed his prime.

Euwe also was self-confident. His lifestyle did not change when he became champion. He kept in top physical condition. His game grew stronger through careful study of the games from the first match. He was fully prepared and had no doubts about his chances, until he saw Alex. This clear-eyed, sun-bronzed man looked far different from what he had remembered. "Alex, how well you look. Where have you been keeping yourself?"

"Oh, I just decided to try a rural life for awhile."

"Well, it's obvious it agrees with you."

It had. The outcome of the match was clear from the beginning. Alex took command at once, and coasted to a win. The final score was 17½ to 12½.

As usual, Euwe was gracious. "Thank you," he said, toasting Alex at the closing banquet. "It was kind of you to lend me your crown for a couple of years, but it is obvious that it is now back where it belongs."

There were other toasts and, after months of abstention, Alex felt entitled to participate fully at every opportunity.

Twenty-seven

"How long will you be gone this time?" Grace asked.

"About three months."

"Three months! Don't you have any idea what is going on? What Germany might do next?"

"Nothing is going to happen." Alex replied. "The danger ended when Hitler took over Czechoslovakia. He made it clear in his agreement with Chamberlain that he had no desire to expand any further. Both Germany and England are sending teams. Our government certainly wouldn't approve and finance our participation if there were the slightest risk. You worry about nothing more than anyone I've ever known. You should come along and enjoy yourself. There will be a lot of entertainment for the wives and opportunities for a lot of sightseeing."

"For three months! No, thanks! Someone has to stay here and take care of things."

"Okay, it's your decision. I won't try to force you."

He would be going back to Buenos Aires. The Eighth Olympiad—the international team competition sponsored by the World Chess Federation—would take place there during the summer of 1939, and Alex was leading the French team.

He had been certain Grace would not accompany him. What was left to their marriage had long been meaningless—loveless sex excepted—but for religious reasons, Grace would not consider divorce, and Alex had no intention of giving up such wealth as came to him through their union. Leaving her at home suited him fine. It was always more rewarding without her around to cramp his style.

There was little likelihood that the French team would win any team prizes. Alex would most probably win the individual prize at the top board, but the rest of the team was not up to the caliber many other nations would bring to the event. Aside from the distasteful prospect of having to sit opposite Capablanca in two games, Alex expected little pressure in this competition. He would not be spending his nights having to prepare for the next day's match. Instead, he was looking forward to the hospitality of Buenos Aires, with its many beautiful and friendly hostesses. He would repay them in the way he knew they would most appreciate.

There were reunions with many of his friends from the twenty-seven nations represented, though neither Marshall nor Lupi were there. The Federation paid all transportation costs, but each nation had to foot the bills for room and board—something that such tiny countries as Latvia, Estonia, Iceland and Palestine had managed, but was beyond the resources of the mighty United States. Alex thought it was disgraceful.

"When will there be a title match?"
"Will it be Capablanca?"
"Is it true that money for the purse has been found?"
"Will it be here in Buenos Aires again?"
"Capablanca charges that you are dodging him. Any comments?"
Alex raised his hands in a gesture of self-defense. Smiling, as he shook his head, he said, "Gentlemen, gentlemen, I've just stepped off the boat. I don't know what may have transpired during my voyage. We're to be here many weeks, and there will be ample time to answer your questions when we know the facts. All I can say at this time is that I am always willing to defend my title against any qualified challenger, provided my published terms for a match are met. I have never dodged a match with anyone, and shall not in the future. I appreciate your interest and will make every effort to keep you informed of developments. I emphasize, however, that I am here as a member of a team representing my country in the Olympiad, and until that competition is completed, my energies will be devoted entirely to getting the best possible score for our team. After that, I can concentrate on questions regarding any possible future match. Now, with your permission, I should like to go to my room and unpack."

The barrage of questions which had confronted him on his arrival came as no surprise. He had dedicated considerable time on the ship to planning his response. It had been almost two years since his return match with Euwe. He had spent much of that time earning what he could through simultaneous exhibitions—some of them blindfold—tournaments, and writing for publications in countries stretching from the Arctic to the Mediterranean. There had been no serious demands for an immediate match. The right of a champion to capitalize on his title for a couple of years was generally accepted.

Now, particularly in Buenos Aires, Alex knew the situation would be different. He would stall as long as he could, but he recognized that public pressure would force a clear answer from him. Luckily, pressure from the media temporarily eased soon after his arrival, when there was confirmation that the United States definitely would not compete. Disappointment and criticism were widespread because the American team had been projected as the probable winner of the Olympiad. There was scathing comment about the "penny-pinching Yankees" on the editorial pages of several important Argentinean papers.

His opponent resigned after fewer than twenty moves. None of his teammates' games were near a conclusion, so he decided on a breath of fresh air. It, too, was brief. The cold wind reminded him that July in Buenos Aires was midwinter. Back inside, as he lit a cigarette, a familiar voice greeted him.

"Alex! How are you?" It was Edward Lasker.

"Ed! How good to see you. I didn't expect to see anyone here from the U.S."

"It was a blow when our team couldn't get any support, but I was going to see this Olympiad, come hell or high water, so I came down at my own expense. How is your team doing?"

"About the way I expected. There are too many teams here with more strength on the third and fourth boards. I guess, with luck, we'll just about break even."

"I suppose the Germans will win it. Don't you agree?"

"If they beat Poland. Without the American team, those two are dominating the field. It would have been a different story if Kashdan, Fine, and the rest of your crew were here."

"Yeah, it really burns me up."

"I haven't heard from Frank in a long time. How is he?"

"Oh, he's the same as ever. Spends most of his time at his own club, pulling his swindles on the innocent."

Alex laughed. "I can imagine! Many's the chap who thought he had a won game against the mighty Marshall, only to see it disappear in a cloud of cigar smoke."

They were walking down the hallway, when Capablanca suddenly appeared, coming toward them. Lasker put out his hand to him, but the Cuban brushed past them as though they weren't there.

"What in the world?" Lasker asked, angrily. "Why did he cut me like that?"

"Because I'm with you. He and I no longer speak. He'll apologize to you later."

"That's a shame. You used to be good friends, I thought. I suppose this is all about the question of another match. May I ask where that stands?"

"I've always been ready to play him again, but he refuses to meet the conditions—the same ones, you know, that he established after he beat Lasker."

Ed looked at him, doubt showing in his eyes. "I'm sure you aren't afraid to play him again, but there have been stories going around which say he has withdrawn all objections to your conditions. Is that true?"

Alex exploded. "I know of only one place on earth where absolute truth might be found, and that's over a chessboard!"

His companion dropped the subject.

Unusual tensions began to appear in the atmosphere at the Olympiad as August moved along. Though the games were still the consuming interest of the participants, the news from Europe was beginning to affect the powers of concentration of many of the Europeans. The Polish team, the only one with a chance to outscore the Germans, met in private, then notified the Olympiad authorities that they would not sit down across from representatives of a nation threatening to invade their homeland. The British team announced that should such an invasion occur, they would immediately withdraw from the competition.

Still sanguine, Alex assembled his team to reassure them. "Don't worry. It's only natural for the Poles to feel uneasy, but when the time comes, they won't give up their chance to beat the German team. As for the British, they're just making a political statement for home consumption. They know that Chamberlain has prevented a war." Satisfied, the team decided against issuing any kind of statement.

Meanwhile, Argentineans had little concern for European squabbles. Those interested in chess kept asking when Capablanca would get the chance to recover the title — something for which he had been waiting twelve years. When the papers revealed that several industrialists had agreed to finance a return match under Alex's conditions, to be held in Buenos Aires, Alex could no longer put off negotiations. At the critical hour, however, rescue came to him, courtesy of Adolph Hitler. Germany invaded Poland.

Wrapping himself in the tricolor, he declared, "Germany has attacked Poland without any justification, and France has responded with a declaration of war. Holding a commission in the French Army Intelligence Service, I have no choice but to return at once for active duty."

It couldn't compare with the better French vintages, but this Argentinean wine wasn't bad, and complemented his dinner nicely. He had to admit that the local beef was superior to the French, and the hotel chef knew his business. His thoughts on such matters were interrupted by the arrival of two visitors.

"Dr. Alekhine? Pardon our intrusion, but may we speak with you?"

"Of course, gentlemen, please sit down. Will you join me in some after-dinner brandy?" he asked, recognizing them as the managers of the Uruguayan and Brazilian teams.

"Thank you. You are most kind."

Alex summoned the waiter, asked for a bottle of brandy and glasses for his guests.

"Now, what can I do for you?" he asked, after their glasses were filled.

The Brazilian said, "Before the unfortunate hostilities erupted in Europe, we had hoped you would be able to honor our country with a visit and some exhibitions. We appreciate your desire to return to France in the near future, but in spite of that, we still hope you might be able to do so by way of Brazil. The trip across the Atlantic from Rio is much shorter than from here, so your date of return should not be much later."

162

Alex emptied his glass, dabbed his lips with his napkin, as he considered the idea. "I think that might be possible. I have not yet received my orders to report for duty. I have pleasant memories of my previous visit to Rio de Janeiro, and I know I would enjoy another, even if it needed to be brief."

The Uruguayan said, "In that case, I would remind you that Montevideo is on the way, and we would feel privileged to have you include an exhibition there also."

"Assuming I can arrange to return home by way of Brazil, I shall be more than pleased to include a stop in Montevideo, a city I have not yet had the opportunity to visit." He refilled the three glasses.

The Brazilian raised his glass. "Let us drink a toast to it happening."

Following the fall of Poland, action was quiet on the western front. France appeared secure behind the Maginot Line, so Alex did not bother to respond to intermittent communications from Grace asking when he would be returning. He gave exhibitions in several Brazilian cities, and then extended his tour to Venezuela and Ecuador.

In early June, Alex was finally on a ship bound from Rio to Lisbon. The German army had made an end run around the Maginot Line, following its lightning conquest of the Low Countries, and it was apparent that France was approaching a state of collapse. Now it was essential to get home without further delay to protect the château and farm. The last cable from Grace had been frantic in tone. The voyage was smooth, but the possibility of the vessel being torpedoed or shelled kept everyone on board in a state of anxiety.

Alex spent only twenty-four hours in Lisbon. Lupi came to the railroad station to see him off.

"Let me know how things go. If the situation becomes unbearable, you will always be welcome here."

The invitation surprised Alex, as he still felt their relationship was in a ticklish state. He embraced Lupi. "Thank you. Your friendship means everything to me, but I hope not to put myself in even further debt to you."

Twenty-eight

Grace opened the door and stared at him, her expression bleak. "At last, when it is too late, who should return but the prodigal."

He walked in, dumped his belongings in the hall, and asked, "What do you mean, too late?"

"The Nazis are taking over the house for use as headquarters for one of their operations. I've been given ten days to move out."

Appalled, he said, "Is there no appeal? Do our authorities have no say in this confiscation?"

"Our authorities? Bah! It was our own Ministry of the Interior which sent me the official notice, just yesterday! The collaborationists pretending to govern France have no power. They just carry out the orders from the Germans."

"They do offer some compensation, don't they?"

"Compensation, my eye! They agree not to shoot us if we are out on schedule. That's our compensation." She glared at him. "It's a shame that the war interrupted your vacation after only six months."

She turned and started to walk away. He reached out, grabbed her shoulder, and spun her around. "Where's the notice?"

She snatched a sheet of paper from the desk and thrust it at him. "Here. Read it and weep! I've already run out of tears."

He read the notice three times, then said, "Before I weep, I'm going to try to do something about this. We won't accept it without a fight."

"Lotsa luck! If you hadn't been gallivanting around, maybe you could have done something useful a month ago, but not now."

He stuffed the document in his pocket, picked up his suitcase, and stomped up the stairs to his room.

164

The following morning, he faced the Deputy Minister of the Interior, whose signature had appeared on the eviction notice.

"May I ask what your interest is in this notice to Madame Wishart, Monsieur Alekhine?"

"She is my wife. I have just returned to France after having been unavoidably detained abroad."

"I see. Unfortunately, our hands are tied in this matter. The German Ministry of Propaganda has ordered that the property be made available for their use."

"From whom did their request come?"

The man behind the desk removed a letter from the file and said, "Here, see for yourself."

Alex read the document. The signature at the bottom attracted his attention. "The man who signed this is at the indicated address?"

"As far as I know. I doubt, however, that you will be able to speak to him."

"Maybe not, but I'll try. Thank you for your cooperation."

"I wish to see Colonel Stellmach."

"Do you have an appointment?"

"No, but if you give him this card, I believe he will see me."

His interrogator disappeared, then returned shortly, followed by the colonel.

"Alekhine! It has been a long time. Come in."

Alex had guessed correctly, that there could not be many Wolfgang Stellmachs, and that he knew the signer of the document he was shown at the Ministry of the Interior. Stellmach was an opponent he had faced more than once in European tournaments.

After they were seated and Alex had accepted a cigarette from him, Stellmach asked, "Now, tell me, what brings you to my office?"

"My home. You are preparing to take it away from us."

"Your home?" I know of no such action. There must be some mistake."

"I certainly hope so. But my wife received an eviction notice from the French Ministry of the Interior stating that you intend to occupy the property for your headquarters."

"No, that is not correct. I know, because I personally looked at the place we will be using. It belongs to an American woman. Her name, as I recall, is Wishart."

"Exactly. Grace Wishart is my wife."

"Your wife? But the name… ?"

"She inherited the château from her previous husband, and that is the name on the deed."

"I see. We visited the property three weeks ago. Why did you wait until now to contact us?"

"I was unavoidably detained abroad and returned only yesterday."

Stellmach frowned, snuffed out his cigarette, shook his head. "It's too bad we couldn't have learned of this sooner. We had an equally suitable alternative location, but it now may be too late to stop the process." He chewed on his lip. "I'll tell you what. My chief is away today, but I will take up the matter with him tomorrow morning. Call me at eleven o'clock, and I will let you know whether anything can be done."

"I suppose the great Alekhine has performed another of his miracles and rescued the house from those thieving bastards?" was her greeting, when he returned.

"Not yet, but there may still be some room for hope. I have a suspicion that the Nazis may be interested in cutting a deal."

"Deal? What kind of deal?"

"I don't know. Let's see what develops over the next few days."

"Something better happen soon. We'll be out on our ears in a week."

"Could you come in tomorrow afternoon, say at 2 o'clock?" Stellmach asked, the next morning, when Alex phoned. "General Gruber said he would like to meet you."

"I'll be there."

General Gruber was a short, slender man, a few years younger than Alex. He had the bearing of one in command of himself, as well as of others.

"I am informed that you have just returned from abroad, Dr. Alekhine. Tell me, how long were you gone, and what were you doing?"

"I have been in South America since early in the summer of 1939. My time has been devoted entirely to the practice of my profession."

166

"You are a chess player, the World Champion?"

"That is correct."

"You had no involvement with the war?"

"None."

"Why not? I understand you are a French citizen. Did you not have talents which could have been useful to the French?"

"I am fluent in a number of languages, and if I had been here at the time the war began, it is possible that I might have been called upon to serve in some capacity."

"Did you not feel it your duty to offer your services?"

"Not particularly. In 1914 I was in Mannheim at the time hostilities started, and was held prisoner for several months, after which I returned to my native Russia where I saw action on the Austrian front and was wounded. My feeling was, and still is, that I have had as much of war as I needed."

"You are a French citizen?"

"Yes."

"Why did you leave Russia?"

"To get away from the Communist butchers who killed my family."

"You feel no ties to the Soviet Union?"

"I loved Russia, but I shall never return there until all of the criminals running the so-called USSR are dead and buried."

A hint of a smile crossed Gruber's face. "That may require some waiting. We have a nonaggression pact with them."

Alex saw no benefit in responding to that statement.

After a final puff of his cigarette, Gruber said, "What is your opinion of the present government of France?"

Alex took some time considering how he wanted to answer. "I have not had time to form any opinion. In any case, if no one bothers me, I don't care who is running the government. I am not a political person. I believe all politicians are only interested in self-aggrandizement. I have traveled in many countries, and it is the same everywhere."

"Then to whom or what are your loyalties?"

"After what I have been through, I feel no obligations to anyone except my wife and myself."

"And that is what brought you to us?"

"I came to try to save our home."

Gruber scratched behind his right ear, as he seemed to study a crack in the wall behind Alex. When he looked at him again, he said, "We could be in a position to respond favorably to your request, but being a pragmatist, I never give something without expecting something in return."

Alex looked straight at him. "That is understandable. I am also a pragmatist. A successful chess player must be."

"Very well. We will have the eviction notice rescinded, and your wife may continue to hold her property, but in return…" and here, Gruber laid out his conditions.

Twenty-nine

It was only a casual game, but a dozen onlookers at the Manhattan Chess Club were watching Capablanca play Isaac Kashdan when a burly figure, who towered over all of them, pushed his way through to the table. It was the editor of the leading American chess journal, a man named Horowitz. "Sorry to interrupt such important goings-on, guys, but I bring momentous news from the battle front."

Kashdan looked up. "Nothing less than Hitler's surrender justifies breaking into this masterpiece I'm creating. It better be important."

Horowitz pulled a chair over to the table, spread out some papers, and said, "Oh, it's definitely more important than that. I have here the latest about our famous French freedom-fighter, the eminent Dr. Alekhine. Guess where he is?"

Capablanca scowled at the mention of Alekhine. "That devil! In hell, I hope, where he belongs."

Horowitz grinned. "You may be near the truth. I've just received a report, with newspaper clippings, which reached me by way of Brazil. For eight months, Alex has been playing in government-sponsored tournaments in Germany and other countries overrun by the Nazis."

The news raised the Cuban's blood pressure to stratospheric levels, and his temper to the boiling point. "That goddamned, lying, hypocritical coward! In Buenos Aires, when the war started, he grabbed the news as an excuse to avoid negotiating a match. 'Duty calls! I must rush back to defend France against the barbarians!' Crap! He dodged me, and he dodged the war for months, hiding out in South America."

"That's right," said Kashdan. "I've heard that he didn't even set foot in France until after the Nazis took Paris."

"Correct, and now we know he has jumped over to what he figures is the winning side," Horowitz added, picking up a news clipping. "But, what you don't know is how far he has jumped. Here come the dirty details."

Several of those standing crowded around him, trying to read over his shoulder.

Horowitz waved the clipping. "Don't bother, unless you can read German. I just brought this as evidence. I've had the articles—there have been three so far—translated, and I'm going to give all of you just a brief summary of some of what it's all about. These are articles published in a number of newspapers in Germany and the occupied countries, and they all carry the name of Alexander Alekhine as their author. They are written as a series titled *Jewish and Aryan Chess*. Being Jewish, I may not be totally unbiased, but I am sure all of you will agree that these are nothing but a load of the worst, vile, lying, monstrous lies ever written!" He stood up, coughing, and got himself some water from a nearby cooler.

The buzz of excited conversation subsided when he resumed his seat. "Okay, don't keep us in suspense," said one of those standing.

"Patience. That's why I'm here. The basic idea he presents in the series is that Jews, by temperament, intelligence, and weakness of character, are unable to play chess at a level comparable with members of the mighty, so-called Aryan race."

"What!" shouted Kashdan. "What the hell's he talking about? Has he forgotten about Lasker and Steinitz, who were world champions?"

"Right. Well, he starts out with the cockeyed theory that 'Jewish' chess thinking is entirely defensive, that Jews lack the courage to play offensively."

Capablanca snorted. "That's the silliest thing I've ever heard, and Alex knows it's hooey. Anyone who played Lasker or read his writings knows better than that."

"Of course, but according to Alex, Lasker just plagiarized Morphy in his books, and that to actually get pleasure from attack was alien to his nature. Along with Steinitz, who he says was the first to demonstrate 'Jewish chess,' he lumps Janowsky, Spielmann—of all people—Rubinstein, Nimzovich, Réti, Flohr, Reshevsky, even Botvinnik. If you can believe his absurd rantings, while they all display some talent for the

170

game, none is an artist, and none has contributed anything original or worthwhile. They all just sit back and wait for their opponent to make a mistake."

"What a load of horse manure!" Kashdan exclaimed.

"And if you think that's offensive, let me tell you what he has to say about that man across the table from you."

Capablanca stared at him, puzzled. "Me?"

"Yeah. He said you started out fine while you were still in Cuba, and had the potential to develop into one of the greatest attacking players of all time. But you made the fatal mistake of enrolling in Columbia University, and exposing yourself to the Jewish influences dominating New York City."

"Why that—" Capablanca appeared to be trying to get up, but he suddenly tilted to one side and fell against the chess table, and then slid to the floor.

By the time the ambulance reached the hospital, the pride of Cuba was dead.

"I don't remember ever hearing you say things like that about those men before the war," said Grace. It was during one of his rare visits home during the past year. "Is it what you really believe?"

"Survival is one of the few things I still believe in," Alex replied. "You have a roof over your head, don't you?"

"And this is why I do?" she asked, holding up the newspaper.

He drained the remaining wine from the bottle, tossed it into the fireplace, and saying, "Think whatever you want," left the room.

❖ ❖ ❖

Sleep without an assist from alcohol was becoming ever more elusive in recent weeks. It had looked like such a sure bet and probably still would turn out right, he kept telling himself, but he couldn't ignore disturbing signs which were beginning to appear. It had looked like a stroke of genius when Hitler turned east and struck a colossal blow at Russia, capturing or killing enormous numbers of troops and destroying vast quantities of military hardware in only a few weeks. Later dispatches, however, had little to say about further advances. Meanwhile, with the entrance of the United States into the conflict, the likelihood of an invasion of Britain had evaporated.

General Gruber had no time for him in recent months, though Stellmach still kept in frequent touch. The tournaments they sponsored attracted favorable comment, particularly when Alex was a participant. The first article he had produced pleased them, Stellmach indicated, though he said Gruber felt that Alex had treated Jewish players somewhat too gently and wanted a change in tone in the next installments.

Pleased with what followed, Stellmach did not object to Alex taking part in a tournament in San Sebastián, a Spanish resort a few miles from the French border. Officially neutral, Spain enjoyed good relations with the Nazis, who were willing to let the Spanish capitalize on the prestige of the world champion on this occasion. After all, Alex had fulfilled his part of the bargain, and certainly would continue to do what was necessary to protect his wife's château.

Alex reached San Sebastián on June 4, 1944. Two days later, the Americans and British landed in Normandy. A week later, Alex crossed the border into Portugal.

Thirty

While sometimes mystified, occasionally disappointed, Alex's actions seldom surprised Lupi any more. Over the years he had learned to recognize and understand—even find justification for—the flaws and inconsistencies in his character, but now, for the first time, he felt sickened.

The strength Alex had shown in rehabilitating himself for the 1937 match with Euwe had impressed him. He was also appreciative, even surprised, by the generosity of the public acknowledgment Alex had made after the match, of how much he was indebted to Lupi for his assistance. He followed the remarkable tournament record of the champion during the next two years with interest and satisfaction. His apparently impeccable public conduct during that period began to persuade Lupi that his opinion of Alex's character weaknesses might no longer be justified.

As reports of events at the Olympiad in Buenos Aires unfolded, though, he knew Alex had not changed. That Alex had used the war as a way to avoid a match with Capablanca did not surprise him. He knew the depths of their mutual antipathy. He was disappointed, though, by Alex's failure to keep his commitment to return promptly to France. When Lupi learned of his presence in Germany he realized that Alex would never feel allegiance to anyone but himself. He had picked the Nazis to win, just as he chose a color on the roulette wheel. His complete lack of principles became clear with the publication of *Jewish and Aryan Chess.*

❖ ❖ ❖

The disgust in Lupi's voice was apparent to Alex. Even so, he persisted. "Antonio, please, I must see you."

Reluctant, but unable to refuse, Lupi said, "I'm tied up in a meeting which will probably go on all afternoon. The earliest I can see you is six-thirty."

"In your office?"

"Yes."

"You are still at the same location?"

"The same."

"I'll be there, and thank you, Lupi."

The nine years had produced changes. Had he himself changed so much? Not in the same way, surely. "I was surprised to receive your call. I thought you were in Germany."

"I was, and I need to explain why."

"You owe me no explanations."

"Yes, I do. I don't care what others think, but your opinions mean much."

Lupi brought a bottle of brandy to the desk. "Drink?"

Alex hesitated, then said, "Yes, please."

Lupi pushed the bottle and a glass over to him. "Help yourself," he said, and lit a cigarette.

Alex poured a half-glassful, tasted it, and said, "Very nice. There's nothing to compare with it in Germany."

Lupi just nodded.

Alex lit his own cigarette, sipped the brandy, then began, "The last time I came to see you, I was a physical wreck, completely out of control. You saved my life, literally, and I am forever in your debt. I may not look much better now, but it is not a physical problem which brings me here."

He drew on his cigarette. "I still have the ability to play winning chess, at least against the opposition available to me, which is not what it was before the war. I am no longer a slave to alcohol, though I sometimes use it to get to sleep."

The ticking of a wall clock seemed louder, as he searched for words.

"I guess I'd better go back to 1939, when I was in Buenos Aires. There was great pressure for another match with Capablanca, and we were negotiating when the war started. I wasn't afraid to play him—or anyone else, for that matter—but the truth is that I hate the man and didn't want to give him the satisfaction."

Lupi said, "Well, that's something you won't need to worry about any more."

"Why not? What do you mean?"

"He's dead. Had a heart seizure last week, while playing at the Manhattan Chess Club."

Thunderstruck, the hand holding his cigarette jerked so hard that a spark landed on the back of his other one. The bottle shook, as he refilled his glass and swallowed the contents without stopping for breath. Ignoring the cigarette still burning in the ashtray, he lit another.

Lupi got another glass, poured himself a small amount of the brandy and pushed the bottle back to Alex.

"I ... I ... I don't know what to say! For twenty years I've detested everything about him, but to hear that he's gone..."

"He was a great master," said Lupi.

"Yes, I don't deny that. One of the greatest."

He rose and began a slow walk from one side of the room to the other. At last, still keeping that pace, he began to speak, almost as much to himself as to the other man. "Yes, he was one of the greatest, but I succeeded in beating him. That's something no one else could do, and no one can ever take that away from me, no matter what. Whatever may have happened since then, the world has to remember who it was that stopped the famous 'chess machine,' and it will. The record is there for the whole world to see, and it can't be erased, the way the Bolsheviks tried to destroy the fact that I ever even existed. The record will also show that I am the only man who ever regained the world championship after losing it. They may not like it, but everyone will have to acknowledge who was the greatest of all time."

He suddenly stopped, looked at Lupi, as though surprised to see him, and stammered, "Forgive me for babbling like this. The news about Capa caught me off balance."

"Yes," Lupi agreed, "maybe I should have broken the news more gently."

Alex started to pour himself some more brandy, but stopped and pushed the bottle away. "No, it wouldn't have made any difference. Let me try to get my thoughts back on track. As I was saying, I was, rather unwillingly, in discussions for another title match when Hitler invaded Poland. Under the circumstances, an immediate return to France seemed appropriate, and offered justification for breaking off match negotiations."

He added another cigarette stub to the growing collection in the ashtray. "I was then persuaded—rather easily, I will admit—that I could have time for some exhibitions and still get home almost as quickly by sailing from Rio de Janeiro. When the Nazis stopped their advance after taking Poland, I convinced myself that they had all they wanted. Besides, I was sure they couldn't crack the French defenses. With that mindset, I no longer felt an urgent need to get home and decided to see more of South America. Since then, I have asked myself many times how I could have overlooked the end run Hitler could make through Belgium and Holland. Or how the French high command could, either. Any chess player would have protected himself against such a flank attack." His head shook in disbelief.

Lupi nodded agreement. "Yes, that was an inexcusable blunder by the French military leaders."

After lighting another cigarette, Alex continued, "When I finally did reach home, I found that the Germans were about to dispossess us of our home. Somehow I was able to reach their propaganda people and offered them a deal. In return for letting us keep our property, I would lend them the prestige of my title by playing in German-sponsored tournaments. They agreed."

He blew an angry plume of smoke at the ceiling. "I'm not proud of what I did, but feel it was the best that I could do in the circumstances. I'm sure it has damaged my reputation in many countries, but what was more important, my reputation or my wife's security?"

"That's a question only you can answer. I will ask you another question, though. Are you now trying to hedge the bet you put on the Axis?"

Alex's smile was sour. "I could never mislead you, could I? You are right, of course. I had the good fortune to be at a tournament in San Sebastián when the British and American offensive began in Normandy. When that happened, I decided to stay away until the dust settles."

"And your wife? How will it affect her?"

"She should be all right unless fighting occurs in the immediate

176

vicinity, which seems unlikely. The Germans will have more pressing things on their minds. Besides, I fulfilled my promises to them. If the Allies succeed in reconquering France, I'm sure they will not give an American property owner any problems.

"So, until the war is settled, what do you figure on doing?"

"It depends. Above all, I want to continue in chess, however I can. Chess is my life. I hope I can earn enough—exhibitions, tournaments, writing, even giving lessons, if I have to."

"It may not be easy. There has been little activity in Portugal since the war started, and the economy is also depressed."

"Even so, I'll find some way to survive." A wry smile crossed his face. "In some ways, my situation here is reminiscent of how it was in 1915, isn't it?"

Lupi meditated, frowning, then said, "Alex, this is something I have to bring up. I have received copies from several sources of recently published articles with you shown as the author. You know which articles I am referring to. What do you have to say about them? Have you completely accepted the Nazi line?"

Alex blinked. "Lupi, I believe that you would not ask such a question if you really thought I could."

Lupi was struck by how the man's eyes suddenly began a constant, rapid blinking. "It's what others are saying."

"I can't help what others choose to think. Each of us has to play the cards fate deals us. Good hands or poor ones, how we play them is what life is all about. With nothing, do we bluff, or do we just fold? If better cards come to us do we gamble for the big prize, or are we content to settle for the smaller but safer reward? Do we cheat? Do we rely on a partner to cover our mistakes? What motivates us?" His breath came in angry spurts, as the blinking accelerated.

Immobile, the man across the desk waited.

"I am aware of the articles people are discussing. My God! I have learned much from the games of Lasker, Steinitz, Nimzovich, and other Jews. I admire their contributions. But since I played in Germany, for the reasons I gave you, I suppose some think I actually could write such rubbish. I won't bother to tell you that I didn't. You will have to decide for yourself whether I could." His blinking was now at a furious rate. He grabbed the bottle for more brandy.

Lupi watched him drink, then said, "What I think isn't the issue. But I'll be surprised if you don't have some problems when the war ends."

Alex slammed his glass on the desk. "Yes, damnit, I'm sure I will, but there is a war on, and I am one of its casualties! So be it. I've survived other wounds and I'll survive this one, too. Trust me."

Lupi laughed to himself. Trustworthiness, he had learned long ago, wasn't exactly Alex's long suit. He stood up. "I need to leave now. When you are settled, let me know what your plans are. I'll keep my eyes open for work opportunities, but they are scarce at present."

"Thanks, and I do thank you for letting me come here and talk. Now, I guess I'd better find a place to stay."

Thirty-one

His reputation and the status of his championship title were being questioned by many chess professionals, and he scoured all the bulletins he could find for hints as to what might happen. Little in his defense was appearing in print. If he had allies, he didn't know where they were. He wasn't finding them at the Lisbon clubs where in earlier years he was always welcomed so warmly.

Little light oozed through the small, grimy window. Whether better illumination would make the place more bearable was debatable. As it was, the tattered bedspread and threadbare rug, main features of the dingy room, were not as noticeable, even when the light was augmented by the solitary, dim, table lamp. With good light, objects to be read needed to be held at arm's length anyway, now that he was in his fifties.

Under the circumstances, to get the news—except for what he absorbed from the tinny voice of the ancient radio the concierge had loaned him, for a consideration—he went elsewhere. What he did read did nothing to diminish the despondency smothering him. The growing sense of optimism he heard expressed in the cafés, bars, or chess clubs, where he spent most of his waking hours, was something he couldn't share. Each new report of the American and Stalinist forces racing to meet somewhere in Germany increased the weight of the worry he carried; he had to keep his apprehension bottled up inside. He could not admit it to Lupi—who undoubtedly knew what was on his mind, anyway—and there was no one else. More than a year had passed without any communication with Grace. Whatever her situation, it was doubtful that she would help him with his coming troubles, even if she could.

Amazingly, it turned out that there were some who were willing to lend a helping hand.

"What's up?" asked Alex, surprised that Lupi had summoned him.

"A piece of mail for you from London, which came in my care."

"London?"

A hint of a smile on his face, Lupi nodded.

The letter was signed by a W. Hatton-Ward, a name he did not recognize. As Alex began to read, he felt his blood surge in the way that champagne does just as the cork escapes the bottle.

Lupi watched the years slide off Alex's face as the content of the letter unfolded. The transformation was startling.

"They invited you, too?" he asked, as Alex looked up from the letter.

Alex could only nod, unable to speak.

"That's good. It gives you a chance to set the record straight."

Alex put the letter down, gripped the edge of the desk to stop his hands from trembling, then fumbled to extract a cigarette from a pack. He looked at it blankly, dropped it on the letter, cleared his throat, and in a shaky voice, asked, "Please, could I have some water?"

Lips trembling, he reached for the water Lupi had poured. He clung to the glass with both hands as he emptied it. He stood up and, still holding it, began moving about, but only in a path which permitted him to keep his eyes on the letter lying there. He began to speak, his voice low at first but gradually becoming stronger. "Lupi, in my life, I haven't always told the truth. There were times when I felt the truth would put me in danger. Other times I felt a lie would be useful to me. There have been times when I distorted or magnified the facts just to amuse myself. I guess I've done that to you, when I thought it was just a harmless joke." His eyes, at last, shifted from the letter and he faced Lupi. "I doubt that I ever really fooled you. You know me too well."

He became aware of the glass in his hands, put it down. The cigarette he had put in the ashtray when he began to read the letter still burned but, ignoring it, as well as the one he had dropped, he took another from his pack and lit it. "We haven't talked much in awhile, but I'm sure you know how worried I've been about my future status in the chess world. Whatever the facts, I'm sure there are those who want to destroy me because I played in German-sponsored events during the war.

180

I don't want to overdramatize it, but there are times when I think about whether I could do away with myself if I were rejected. I believe I would. Life would be meaningless."

He sat down, extinguished both cigarettes. "I've never told you, but I was once sentenced to death, and was given a reprieve only at the last hour."

The unexpected disclosure startled Lupi. "What!"

"It's something I've never told anyone, except Nadyezhda, but it is the absolute truth. It was a terrifying experience which still gives me nightmares, years later. I can't describe how I felt when I learned that I would be freed. I am telling you this now, because it is the only way I can explain what this invitation means to me. It is the second time my life has been spared."

Lupi was further astounded to see Alex fumble for a handkerchief, as tears began to run down his cheeks. Reacting to the sight, he poured brandy into a glass and pushed it across the desk.

Alex drank, then said, "Sorry to make a spectacle of myself."

"No apology needed. I can appreciate how you must feel."

Alex put down the empty glass. "Will you go to London, too?"

"No. They were nice enough to invite me, but since I no longer hold the Portuguese title, I am giving up international competition. I'm getting too old for it."

"You're no longer champion? I didn't know."

Lupi grinncd. "Ycs, but at least, it's still in the family. My nephew Francisco now carries the banner. He will be our only representative in London."

"I'll look forward to meeting him. I am surprised, though, at your decision. That's something I could never do. I must compete as long as I live."

"After more than forty years, there's not enough fire left in me. I'm sure, though, that you'll never give up."

Alex finished his brandy, and shook his head when Lupi offered more. "No, thank you. I'm going to my room to write my acceptance to Hatton-Ward. Will it be all right if he continues to write to me in your care?"

"Of course."

Alex prepared to leave, then, obviously embarrassed, said, "When

I'm ready to go to London, could you lend me some money, to be paid back from my prize money?"

"That's no problem. Would you like it now?"

"No thanks. I believe I can manage my present expenses."

The invitation was to a "Victory Tournament," which would be held in London in January 1946. To celebrate peace, the British Chess Federation hoped to bring together the best players from all over the world—although it was questionable whether Russia would send any. Following Alekhine's defection a quarter-century back, the Soviets were still leery about letting any of their masters outside their borders.

As Alex had reason to fear, the matters of his participation in Nazi-sponsored tournaments and whether he actually was the author of the infamous articles did come up with the tournament planning committee, and were the subjects of vigorous debate. In the end, though, traditional British views of sportsmanship prevailed. After all, as Hatton-Ward put it, their objective was to bring about a competition of the strongest players—and Alekhine's absence would diminish it, since he was still the world champion. It was not the committee's function to sit in judgment on anyone.

It would not be that simple, however, as he had to explain, when he reassembled the committee for an emergency meeting.

"I fear we are confronted by a sticky situation. The United States Chess Federation has cabled us that it would not pay the expenses of, nor sponsor, any American if Dr. Alekhine is a participant."

There were sounds of protest from the committee. Who did the Americans think they were, dictating who we can invite?

Hatton-Ward shook his head. "They are not the only ones. Professor Euwe has also sent word that he will not attend if Alekhine is here. As you are well aware, we have been counting on the Americans to send at least a half-dozen players of the caliber of Euwe. Without them, the strength and prestige of the competition slips to the point where our tournament sponsors will withdraw their support, and the entire thing will surely collapse. I see no alternative but to bow to the inevitable. The invitation to Dr. Alekhine must be canceled."

182

With regret the committee concurred unanimously, leaving Hatton-Ward with the painful task of notifying Alekhine of their decision.

When Lupi learned of their action, he hurried to Alex's lodgings, concerned about his state of mind. If Lupi had hoped to raise his spirits, it was a wasted effort. Alex was in a state of belligerent drunkenness, which soon changed to one of self-pitying tears. Unable to reason with him in any way, he left in disgust.

Keeping him out of the tournament was not enough for the anti–Alekhine faction. At the conclusion of the competition in London, thirty-four of the leading masters of the chess world convened to consider further action. Euwe served as their chairman. Following hours of heated argument, a majority approved a compromise resolution. It stated that evidence of the nature of his collaboration with the enemy required investigation by the authorities in France, that Alekhine should make himself available to them for that purpose, and that the World Chess Federation should act to expedite the process. A copy of the resolution was sent to Alex.

The hole-in-a-wall café would never be included in a list of Lisbon's recommended eating establishments, but Alex had discovered that it did serve a generous bowl of nourishing soup for a reasonable price. This was important, as his diminishing resources had to be conserved. He emptied the bowl, then wiped it dry with a piece of bread, which he chewed with caution to avoid as much pain as possible from his few remaining teeth. He was again suffering the penalty of years of dental neglect.

From the inside pocket of his spotted and fraying jacket he retrieved his copy of the resolution and read it for the twentieth time. Its words burned in his brain, and their heat traveled to his gut, where the fire was unceasing. He clenched his hand, crushing the document into a ball, then spread it on the table, smoothed it, and returned it to his pocket.

His hand trembling, he lit one of his few remaining cigarettes and reached for the copy of a morning paper someone had abandoned on an adjoining table. Alex turned the pages aimlessly, until his eyes spotted her picture. Except for that one brief glimpse years ago—before the war—he hadn't seen her in thirty years, but recognition was instantaneous. Under the picture the text read:

> For the first time in a decade, citizens of Lisbon will have the opportunity to hear Rosa Pereira, Portugal's premier violinist, in concert with the Lisbon Philharmonic Orchestra, Friday and Saturday nights of this week.
> After many years of performances, principally in South America, England and France, she has been limiting herself to just a dozen or so concerts a year, preferring to spend most of her time at her home in Mallorca.
> At a reception in her honor, this afternoon, at the Avenida Palace Hotel, official recognition of her outstanding career will be offered by representatives of various elements of the community.

He checked the date to be certain it was the current day's newspaper, paid his bill, bought another package of cigarettes, and walked to and stood across the street from the Avenida Palace Hotel. The rays of the mid-afternoon sun did little to counteract a persistent wintry breeze. The few pedestrians on the avenue hurried along, not pausing to look in the windows of the expensive shops of the neighborhood. Pacing back and forth from time to time, Alex was glad that he was wearing his heavy coat.

Midway through his third cigarette, he watched a crowd of well-dressed people begin to emerge from the hotel. Most of them rode away in chauffeur-driven cars, some in taxis. As the crowd thinned, he crossed the street and stopped near the hotel entrance. His patient vigil was rewarded when Rosa Pereira came out with two other women. After chatting briefly, the two kissed her and left in a taxi. As Rosa turned to reenter the hotel, she felt a hand on her arm, and a voice said, "Rosa?"

Her face blanched as she turned and, despite the changes, recognized him. She jerked away.

"Please," he appealed, "just give me a minute." Distress evident in his voice, anguish in the bloodshot eyes, disintegration dominant everywhere in the once-handsome face.

"Well?" she said, backing away a couple of feet.

"Truly, I just wanted to greet you, and to inquire about your mother."

"My mother!" The sudden distortion of her face was startling. "All right, I'll tell you about my mother. Can you still remember that park up the hill from our house, the one the three of us walked to one Sunday? The park with the wall over which there was the marvelous view of the water, with the rocks far below? Three days after you deserted her, my mother's body was found on those rocks." A sob slipped past her fierce voice. "In the house was a note she had written, taking the blame for what she felt had wrecked our lives, and begging for my forgiveness. As for me, I have never forgiven myself for my immature behavior, and for not returning to tell her how much she meant to me and how foolish we both were to destroy ourselves for a lying opportunist like you!" Tears streaming down her face, she dashed into the hotel.

Alerted by the stridency of Rosa's voice, the hotel doorman kept an eye on the man who stood there, apparently paralyzed by the impact of whatever she had said. At last, Alex walked away, at first without purpose, then with a fixed objective.

His steps took him up the hill to the house where he had stayed. There was a different name at the gate but, otherwise, little evidence of change. After regaining his breath, he continued up the winding path to the park and made his way to the stone wall. He leaned against it, his chest hurting with each rasping breath of cold air. Loath to do so, he made himself look over the edge down to the jagged rocks more than a hundred feet below, as he tried to digest the idea of emulating Maria's plunge. Eyes closed, Alex tried to imagine the horrifying sensation of dropping through space. Could he do it? Would he? Tears began to leak from between his lids. Shuddering, he backed away and began a slow, stumbling meander back to his lodgings.

The concierge accosted him when he walked in. "There is a message for you," he said. "A Mr. Lupi has asked that you call him immediately. He said the matter is urgent."

When the words penetrated, he was surprised. This was the first communication from Lupi in months. He hadn't seen him since the London tournament disaster. "May I use your telephone?"

The concierge handed it to him, and he placed the call. "Lupi? What's up?"

"Alex, come to my office immediately. Something important has happened!"

"What?"

"Don't ask. Just get here!"

Alex went to his room first to wash his face, then made his way to Lupi's office.

He opened the door without knocking. "What's this all about?"

The haunted eyes in the ravaged face appalled Lupi, erased the grin with which he started to greet him. "Hello, Alex, sit down. Can I get you something to drink?"

"No," he said, shaking his head. He slumped into a chair. "What's so urgent?"

"Read this," was the answer.

Alex examined the cable. It was addressed to Lupi, signed J. N. Derbyshire, President, British Chess Federation.

> Please help us transmit message to Dr. Alekhine that Moscow Chess Club has issued challenge for world chess title match between Mikhail Botvinnik and Alekhine to be held in London under British sponsorship. Moscow guarantees 2500 Pounds Sterling with 1500 to winner and 1000 to loser plus funds to cover all necessary expenses of contestants.

Expression frozen, Alex stared at the piece of paper. He read it a second time, his head shaking in disbelief.

Lupi watched him, then brought a bottle of brandy and glasses from a cabinet. "Don't you agree that this calls for a drink?"

Alex accepted the glass, gulped its contents while his eyes remained glued to the cable. "I can't believe this. It has to be a trick. For years they have done everything within their power to deny my very existence. Now they recognize my title and offer me money to play one of their own?" He pushed his glass across the desk.

Lupi poured more brandy for him and said, "I don't think it is a trick. Their objectives seem quite obvious to me. They know that the rest of the world would like to withdraw recognition of you as champion, but the Russians are shrewd enough to know that handing the title to anyone who hadn't beaten you would be a hollow action. They believe that Botvinnik can do it, and have decided to strike while the others dither. If he wins from you, everyone will have to admit he is the world champion. Doesn't that make sense?"

Alex frowned, swallowed more of the brandy. "I suppose so," his voice doubtful.

The absence of enthusiasm puzzled Lupi. He had never seen Alex quite this way. "Is there something else troubling you? I was expecting you to be jumping for joy. A match with Botvinnik should mean a lot more for you than any tournament could. Besides, the willingness of the British Federation to sponsor it will spike the guns of your critics."

"Yes, you are right, as usual. And there is something else. The truth is, I've had a very traumatic experience today, and am still having trouble concentrating on anything, even something as important as this."

"Would it help if you told me about it?"

"Thanks, but no. It is something I'll have to deal with on my own." He finished what was left in his glass. Then, a trace of a smile appearing for the first time since entering the room, he said, "Of course, I should be overjoyed, and maybe I will start to feel that way in a little while. At the same time, I realize that I'm not ready for a match." Humble, he said, "I know I haven't acted recently in a way to deserve any more support from you. Even so, and I know it is asking a lot, if you can, and if you believe I really could be successful against Botvinnik, I would be forever grateful for any help you could give me to prepare, and would be honored if you would again agree to serve as my second."

Lupi lit a cigarette. It was a long time before his answer came. "Okay, Alex, even though there are still some unanswered questions in my mind. I know you have been through a bad time, so I will try to help you prepare. If you show that you are as serious about this match as you were the last time, I'll also act as your second."

Almost in tears, Alex gripped Lupi's hand in both of his. "Thank you! Thank you! There has never been anyone as generous as you. What else can I say? I can never thank you enough."

Lupi relieved the tension with a chuckle. "One reason I'll help is because I don't want to see the Commies win."

For the first time in many days, Alex laughed. "Neither do I." Hand shaking from emotion, he managed to light a cigarette and inhaled deeply. The voice, sober, said, "It seems I've been indebted to you ever since we met. Now, I need to ask for two more favors. First, would you please cable Derbyshire that I accept the challenge and suggest that the match begin five months from now. Second, my resources have been stretched to the limit. Does your offer to lend me money still stand? You'll get it back from my share of the purse."

"Of course. How much will you need?"

Walking back in the darkness, the idea that he would have this new opportunity for redemption took hold, wiping away memories of the earlier events of the day. There was a spring in his step and the skies seemed to clear.

He greeted the concierge like an old friend and handed him some bills. "I'm celebrating tonight. Please order me a steak dinner and a bottle of the best red wine delivered to my room as soon as possible. Keep whatever is left for yourself."

His room was not the beneficiary of the trickle of heat emerging from the ancient furnace system. Alex still wore his hat and overcoat when the meal was delivered. It was placed on the table beside the chessboard where he was already looking at variations of one of his favorite openings.

It wasn't until his jaws closed on the first bite of steak that his euphoria subsided as he was reminded of the state of his teeth.

Thirty-two

As soon as Alex had left him, Lupi cabled Derbyshire that Alex accepted the challenge. That chore out of the way, he sat, swirling brandy in his glass, trying to understand himself. How could he agree to help someone he was certain was guilty of such loathsome acts? Why was he always unable to refuse whatever Alex asked? Did he subconsciously accept the role of a parent shielding a wayward child from the consequences of his actions? When he persuaded Alex to remain in Lisbon in 1914 did he become responsible for all of his future behavior? The chimes of a clock interrupted those thoughts. He had to hurry or would be late for a concert date with a friend.

J. N. Derbyshire read Lupi's cable with pleasure, promptly had the message transmitted to Botvinnik, and called on several associates to meet the following afternoon to plan arrangements for the match. He also notified London newspapers of the coming event.

Muttering against fate—personified by the sergeant who had sent him out into the blustering, strange blend of sleet and sunshine—the young policeman trudged to his assigned destination. It was a relief to get into the warm lobby. Before he could turn down his coat collar, the concierge, pale-faced, rushed up. "Police? Thanks for coming so quickly!"

He cleared his throat. "Yes. What's the problem?"

"I'd better show you. It's upstairs. Come along, too, Paolo," he said to a young man at the foot of the stairs leaning over the balustrade as though about to be sick.

The concierge opened the door of a second-floor room and stood aside.

It was the first time in his four months on the force that the policeman had ever encountered a dead person. He stopped short, swallowed hard, moved closer to stare briefly at the body, then backed out into the hall where the others stood. "Who found him?"

"Paolo," said the concierge, pointing to him.

"How did that happen?" he asked the trembling youth in a stern voice, while trying to mask his own reactions to what he had just seen.

"The tray wasn't out in the hall, and there was no answer to my knock, so I went back down for the key."

"Tray?"

The concierge spoke up, "Dr. Alekhine, the man in there, ordered dinner served in his room last night. When finished, he should have put the tray of dishes outside his room."

The police officer glanced back at the table, "It looks like he didn't get to eat much before it happened."

"That's right," agreed the concierge.

"What do you know about him? How long has he been staying here?"

"He's been here a number of months. He said he was a professional chess player and claimed to be the world champion. It seemed to me that he was down on his luck. He struck me as a very moody person and usually had very little to say. A lot of the time it was clear that he was quite drunk."

"Did you see other people with him?"

"Not lately. Another guy, very prosperous-looking, used to visit him sometimes, but I haven't seen him in several months, and I never saw anyone else with him." The concierge hesitated, then added, "Oh, yes, he did get what seemed to be an urgent phone call yesterday. I gave him the message when he came in about four o'clock. He returned the call at once, and went out again a short time later. When he got back a couple of hours later, he seemed excited and happy, and ordered dinner to be sent to his room."

"Do you know who called him?"

"I have a name and number down at my desk."

"Let's go see it."

The policeman called his sergeant, giving him a summary of what he had seen and learned.

"Okay," said the sergeant, "stay put and keep the room secure until I get there. I'll call the coroner." He hung up the phone and went to see the captain in charge of the station.

The captain gave a low whistle. "Alekhine? Yes, I know who he was. And that caller, Lupi? I wouldn't be surprised if he is part of the winery Lupis. You'd better take charge, and handle this with kid gloves. I'll take care of the press."

He would, thought the sergeant. Big stories were always in the captain's domain.

Lupi returned from lunch to find a message to phone the sergeant as soon as possible. He recognized the number as the one he had used the previous day. Perturbed, he called at once. "Sergeant, this is Antonio Lupi, returning your call."

"Yes, sir. Thank you for responding promptly."

"What can I do for you?"

"Did you leave a message here yesterday for a Dr. Alekhine?"

"Yes, I wanted to see him."

"And did you?"

"Yes, he came to my office in the afternoon. Why do you ask?"

"Well, sir, I'm sorry to inform you that Dr. Alekhine has died."

"Died? I don't understand. He was fine when he left here."

"What time was that?"

"Late afternoon, shortly after five-thirty, I believe. What happened? Was he in an accident?"

"We don't have the answer yet. We are waiting for the coroner."

"Where is he?"

"In his room. Do you know where that is?"

"Yes, I've been there."

"Would it be possible for you to come here to confirm the identification and, possibly, to provide other information which might help us with our investigation?"

"Of course. I can be there in half-an-hour."

Lupi's thoughts were in turmoil as he drove. He had long wondered what the eventual solution would be to Alex's problems but, despite his drinking, the possibility of death was something he never considered seriously. Recalling his reference yesterday to a traumatic experience, Lupi wondered if that might have some connection with his death. If so, it couldn't have produced suicide—not with the Botvinnik match in the offing.

The concierge signaled to the sergeant when Lupi walked in. Relieved, he pulled away from several reporters and greeted Lupi. "Thank you for coming. Let's go upstairs."

One of the reporters recognized Lupi and tried to question him.

"I'm sorry, but I just learned of this tragic event, and can tell you nothing about it."

"Could you give us some background about…"

The sergeant interrupted, "Sorry, but you'll have to wait. At the moment we need Mr. Lupi's assistance."

The door to the room was open but, except for two policemen on guard, the hall was empty. Inside a police photographer was taking pictures of the scene and others were taking notes.

Lupi paused at the door and took a deep breath before following the sergeant into the room. Half the floor space was filled by a bed, dresser and armoire. Centered in the remaining space was a table, half-covered by dishes of uneaten food. A chessboard with pieces set up in an end game position took up the rest of the table surface. Still wearing a hat and overcoat, Alex sat, sightless eyes fixed on the game.

"That's how we found him," said the sergeant. "He hasn't been moved, and won't be until the coroner sees him. You confirm that it is Alekhine?"

Lupi nodded as he backed out of the room, anxious to escape the cloying odor, and wishing he could erase the sight from his memory.

The sergeant followed. "Did he have a family?"

"A wife who is in France." He hesitated, then said, "Would you like for me to notify her?"

"We'd appreciate that, and also if you could learn her wishes about arrangements."

Lupi nodded. "Is there anything else?"

"Not at this time. Thank you very much for your help."

Appalled and still shaken by the sight in the room, his only response to the waiting group of reporters was, "Gentlemen, the world has lost a genius and I have lost a friend of thirty years." With that, he drove away.

"Hello?"

"Grace? This is Antonio Lupi."

"Lupi? Where are you? Why are you calling?"

"I'm sorry, but Alex is dead."

"Dead! What are you saying? What happened?"

"He was found in his room this morning. They don't know what happened, but the police are investigating."

"Police? Why are they investigating?"

"I'm not sure, but I think that's routine when the cause isn't known. They will be waiting for a report from the coroner."

"Had he been sick?"

"Not that I was aware of."

She was silent for a moment. "I guess his drinking had something to do with it."

"Possibly," he replied, "though he was sober when I saw him yesterday."

"Well, that's something I hadn't seen in years."

Lupi drew a deep breath. "The police would like to know your wishes about his burial."

She snorted. "My wishes? Mr. Lupi, for all practical purposes, our marriage ended years ago. I don't give a damn what they do with him. I just don't want his body shipped here. Thank you for calling me." She hung up before he could find words.

Derbyshire and his committee were deep in discussions about match arrangements when he stood to accept another cable from Lupi. "Good Lord!" he gasped, sinking back into his chair. "This is unbelievable! Alekhine is dead!"

Word flashed around the world following Alex's death on March 23, 1946. Initial wire service reports were brief, but longer obituaries, full of details about his background, his professional accomplishments, and the controversies swirling around his wartime activities, plus the surprising additional news from England about the proposed match with Botvinnik, appeared during the days which followed. Scattered in these were a variety of rumors — fueled by comments and conjectures from various elements of the chess community — as to the cause of death: heart attack, cirrhosis, suicide because of gambling losses or the demands that he face the French authorities, even that he was the victim of deliberate poisoning.

A few days later, the coroner, a friend of his, called Lupi. "Antonio, I thought you'd want to be the first to know. Your friend, Alekhine, died of strangulation."

"Strangulation! How? Are you saying it was murder?"

"No, no, nothing like that. He choked to death because of a piece of meat stuck in his throat. It was three inches long, and unchewed."